ROCK MY WORLD

ROCK MY WORLD

A Novel of Thongs, Spandex,
and Love in G Minor

LIZA CONRAD

nal
jam
books

NAL JAM
Published by New American Library, a division of
Penguin Group (USA) Inc., 375 Hudson Street,
New York, New York 10014, USA
Penguin Group (Canada), 10 Alcorn Avenue, Toronto,
Ontario M4V 3B2, Canada (a division of Pearson Penguin Canada Inc.)
Penguin Books Ltd., 80 Strand, London WC2R 0RL, England
Penguin Ireland, 25 St. Stephen's Green, Dublin 2,
Ireland (a division of Penguin Books Ltd.)
Penguin Group (Australia), 250 Camberwell Road, Camberwell, Victoria 3124,
Australia (a division of Pearson Australia Group Pty. Ltd.)
Penguin Books India Pvt. Ltd., 11 Community Centre, Panchsheel Park,
New Delhi - 110 017, India
Penguin Group (NZ), cnr Airborne and Rosedale Roads, Albany,
Auckland 1310, New Zealand (a division of Pearson New Zealand Ltd.)
Penguin Books (South Africa) (Pty.) Ltd., 24 Sturdee Avenue,
Rosebank, Johannesburg 2196, South Africa

Penguin Books Ltd., Registered Offices: 80 Strand, London WC2R 0RL, England

First published by NAL JAM, an imprint of New American Library,
a division of Penguin Group (USA) Inc.

First Printing, June 2005
10 9 8 7 6 5 4 3 2 1

NAL JAM and logo are trademarks of Penguin Group (USA) Inc.

LIBRARY OF CONGRESS CATALOGING-IN-PUBLICATION DATA:
Conrad, Liza.
   Rock my world : a novel of thongs, spandex, and love in G minor / Liza Conrad.
      p. cm.
   ISBN 0-451-21523-0 (trade pbk.)
   1. Rock musicians—Family relationship—Fiction. 2. Fathers and daughters—Fiction. 3.
Internship programs—Fiction. 4. Teenage girls—Fiction. 5. Rock groups—Fiction. I. Title.
   PS3603.O5566R63 2005
   813'.6—dc22   2005000003

Set in Melior
Designed by Elke Sigal

Printed in the United States of America

Acknowledgments

I'd like to thank my agent, Jay Poynor of the Poynor Group, for always watching out for me and for being a friend, as well as an agent.

A special thank-you to my editor, Anne Bohner. I admire your vision and energy and focus, and I'm grateful you embraced this concept. I'm appreciative of the team at NAL/Penguin, from cover designers to marketing, for getting the allure of rock and roll.

I would like to thank Kerri Berryman for letting me use her daughter's name as my main character. And to "Livy" for being one of the coolest kids I know.

A thank-you for my "teen expert," Alexa Milo, who made sure my characters talked like teenagers. And for being someone I am really proud to know—you are such a special teen, as well as musician.

As always, a thank-you to my supportive family and friends, and a special thank-you to Jon Van Zile for helping me get on track as far as the music. Thanks, too, to Pammie and Gina, as always. Our writing group remains so important to my writing—and my life.

To Meredith Krashes for loving Bruce Springsteen as much as I do. Growing up we all have a soundtrack to our adolescence, and ours was always the Boss.

And last but not least, to J.D. for putting up with this rebel rock and roll lover even when I am a one-woman writing hurricane and operating on no sleep and a lot of Coke and sushi.

Chapter One

"Rock 'n' Roll Lifestyle"

—Cake

And on the sixth day, God created Nick Hoffman's voice, Liz Phair's lyrics, Kurt Cobain's angst, and Lenny Kravitz's guitar licks. And he saw that it was good. So He just said, "Screw it . . . tomorrow I'm resting."

I looked across the table at Carl Erikson, *Rock On* magazine's editor in chief, as he put down my essay called "The Creation of Rock and Roll" that had run in my high school newspaper. I held my breath.

"This is really quite clever, Livy," he said.

I relaxed a little. "Clever" is a lot better than "What were you thinking, slacker?" or "Cheesy"—and I so wanted this summer gig. I tried to picture Carl forty pounds lighter. With hair. And an earring. In tight jeans. With eyeliner. Back when he was cool, or at least not bald and "pleasantly plump," back when he and my father used to hang out after Babydolls' concerts and smoke an ungodly amount of pot. And Lord knows what else. Trying not to laugh at the image, I simply said, "Thanks."

One time, my father said, when I was four years old, Carl stripped naked and played air guitar in our living room during a party. I don't remember that, which is just as

1

well. If I'd been able to recall Carl's flaccid—my father remembers that detail perfectly—penis, I was quite positive I would have fallen on the floor in hysterics and wouldn't have been able to do the interview.

"You know what we're asking you to do, right?" Carl raised an eyebrow, his reading glasses perched on the end of his nose.

I nodded.

"Good," he said. "I like the way you write. At seventeen, you're better than half of my staff, and I mean that—though don't tell them or I'll have a mutiny on my hands. *Rock On* is for the MTV set. We're not like *Rolling Stone*. They cover the whole spectrum, and they're oh-so-self-important." He took his glasses off and laid them on his desk. "We want readers mostly your age . . . and into their twenties. We've got gossip and lots of photos. Backstage candids. Interviews with actors. Do you read *Rock On*?"

I nodded, even though I didn't. I thought most of it was crap.

"Of course you do. All teens in your age bracket do."

"Sure," I said convincingly.

"Well . . ." Carl leaned back in his enormous leather chair, a view of the New York skyline behind him. "I don't have to tell you what the Babydolls mean to rock-and-roll history. I'm sure you meet people all the time who tell you what an amazing musician and singer your father was—and is. And the reunion tour is going to be the hottest summer stadium ticket both here and in Europe."

"And Japan," I said. "That's where the tour starts."

"Yeah. The Japanese love them. And now he's got that

2

American Express commercial. Hysterical. Comes across as über-hip. And with the Wolves opening for the Babydolls on the tour . . . Jesus, I wish I was twenty again." He smiled, and for a split second I could see the twenty-year-old Carl. His eyes were less tired, and his dimples showed.

"Well, Livy, I'm sold. What I want is a series of . . . you could make them like journal entries . . . from the road. Places like Madison Square Garden, L.A., London. Wherever they are—wherever you are. And then mingled with that, I'd love to read the story of the Babydolls, your life with your parents and the band and so on. I'd love to connect this tour with readers your age—they'll be able to relate to you."

"Like Kelly Osbourne without the pink hair. And the foul mouth—most of the time."

"Yeah. Minus the pink hair and the F-word." He smiled at me. "I like how you think. You're quick—like your old man. I'll give you my e-mail, and Rob's—he's a very sharp editor. He's good, and he's excited about this."

"Great."

"I'd also like you to take digital pictures—candids—of the tour bus, the jet, the crowds, the band, the Wolves."

The Wolves were opening for my father's band. Nick Hoffman was so good-looking that grown women got wolf-paw tattoos on their breasts. I remember being five or six and seeing women throwing baby-doll pajamas on the stage at my father. Though tossing underwear and pajamas, and permanently inking your body seem like two entirely different brands of fan obsession.

"Sure." Photograph Nick Hoffman? I could just imagine my best friend, Cammie, when she heard that: *Can we take his picture with his shirt off?*

"One story a week for the summer tour. Put you on the payroll for two hundred a week; fifty bucks for every photo we use."

"Deal." I said it calmly, but I would have done the stories for free—just to start building up press clippings. My dream was to someday start my own rock magazine. Getting *paid* to write? That meant I could actually *say* I was a writer. For real.

Carl stood and shook my hand, then came out from behind the desk. Suddenly, and without warning, he enveloped me in a bear hug. "God, I remember when you used to toddle around the house in your diapers. Can't believe it. You look like a model, and you're taller than I am."

"That's not hard, Carl," I said, looking down at the top of his bald head. I'm five-foot-eleven. He had to be five-foot-five.

He laughed and put his arm around me.

"So you think if I was as tall as your dad, *I* would have gotten all the groupies?"

"Not unless you put on some spandex back then."

"Oh, I had spandex."

"Well, you know how girls dig musicians. And you can't play anything," I teased.

"I once played the tambourine onstage with the Babydolls. At Wembley."

We left his office in search of my father.

"Tambourines don't count."

"Yeah, well, I had hair then, too." He looked over at me and winked.

Down the hall, I heard females giggling. Lots of them. Along with a cooing sort of fawning noise. It could only be my dad—women still fall all over him. He says it's because he kicked hard drugs, so he didn't age like Keith Richards, the walking cadaver—though that's giving cadavers a bad name. They don't make the corpses on *CSI* appear that bad. My father still looks young. He wears his hair to his shoulders, and it's as thick and dirty blond as when he was twenty-one. He has blue eyes and a lanky build, and he speaks with a raspy voice, like some late-night deejay who's chain-smoking through his night shift. He wears boot-cut jeans, custom-made lizard-skin cowboy boots, and tight black T-shirts that show off his body. He looks, all the time, like what he is: a rock star. All my life, girls tried to be friends with me because of him. It's beyond creepy to go to a friend's house and see a poster of your father in her bedroom—when you know in her fifth-grade mind she's fantasizing about kissing him. *Gross!*

Carl opened the door to *Rock On*'s conference room. And there was my dad, Paul James, black Sharpie pen in hand, signing the left breast of some woman, her top unbuttoned to her belly button. She blushed and covered up. The other women were laughing. Not just women my dad's age either. There were interns who looked just a couple of years older than I am—college girls. I rolled my eyes, and Dad came over and kissed me.

"Well, baby?"

Carl smiled. "She's hired. We worked it all out. Have some paperwork to fill out, but it's all set."

"Cool. That's my girl."

We hung around the office, took care of the paperwork, and then Dad and I went downstairs, where our limousine waited. My father got his fifth DUI before I was even in junior high. After that, he never bothered to get his license back again. It's kind of pathetic when you have to drive your own parents around. My mother's from England, and she never did learn to operate a car on our side of the road. What a pair they are. At least, however, I have a convertible. I mean, if you have to chauffeur your father around, you might as well drive something you're not embarrassed by. And when I'm not at the wheel, then it's the limo. Toby is our driver/bodyguard. He used to take me to school every day until I got my license. He also keeps all the liquor in the house under lock and key.

In the back of the limousine, Dad grinned. He has this lopsided smile women have been swooning over forever. I think that's half the reason Mom married him.

"You're all grown-up, Livy."

I rolled my eyes. "*Please* don't get all mushy on me."

"Well, it seems like yesterday. I mean, holy shit, I can barely remember you when you were small. And now you've got your first job as a real writer. Next thing it'll be college. One year to you going off to school. Just one more year. Then next thing you know you'll be hosting *Total Request Live.*"

"Dad, I'm a writer, not a TV host. They read cue cards."

"Well . . . where did the time go? You make me feel damn old, Liv."

"The time went down the sucking vortex of drugs, Dad. You can't remember stuff because you pretty much went through the 1990s in a blackout."

"Ahh, yes. Because we can't have a conversation without you reminding me of that. And now, unfortunately, I'm constantly aware that you're way too clever with words, courtesy of that very expensive private school you go to. Lucky me . . . now you can mouth off, and I get to remember it all because I have no blackouts to help me forget you're a pain-in-the-ass teenager instead of the sweet little girl I used to carry around backstage." He sighed. "Anyway, I'm sober now."

"Yes. Now."

"What's that supposed to mean?"

"Dad, sometimes it seems as though you don't really think things through. Have you thought about this tour, Dad? About going back out on the road? I mean, really thought about it?"

"Yeah. At least I think so. Why?"

"Sex, drugs, and rock and roll, Dad. You're going back on tour with Greg Essex and Steve Zane, neither of whom has ever met a drug he didn't like. And you and Charlie have been trying to go to AA. I mean, it's just getting so Mom and I don't have to worry about you. Have you thought about what the tour bus is going to be like? What backstage is going to be like? Not to mention the whole Paris incident. The stuff of legend, Dad. Are you sure you can handle this?"

"Who's the parent here?"

"That's debatable."

"Well, since when did you get so smart?"

"Since I raised myself. Toby went to more of my school events than you did."

He leaned his head back, shut his eyes, and pretended to sleep. I could see Toby's expression in the rearview mirror and knew he was hoping I'd let it drop. I watched my dad fake-sleeping, trying to remember a time when he was responsible, and pretty much recalling none. We rode back to Nyack in silence, and Toby pulled into the gate and up our long driveway. Dad next pretended to wake up. As we got out of the car, he grabbed my hand.

"I love you, Livy. You're my girl and always have been. I hate fighting."

"I know."

Dad let go of my hand and went into the house. I got my purse, feeling aggravated. I was one of those big "surprises" in life. Mom was a backup singer who had fallen in love—like the whole world—with Greg Essex, lead guitarist of the Babydolls, who had the biceps and forearms of a sex god. They were together first; then he broke her heart when he suggested a threesome with another woman. She ran into the arms of his best friend, my father and the band's lead singer, and five months later—just starting to show—my mother married my dad. There was some question about my paternity, but I happen to have my father's blue eyes. They are this weird icy blue. And I'm his. Much as I sometimes wish I weren't.

Our house—for a couple who never had any other children—is way too big. Rock-star big. Eight bedrooms. Which is okay, I guess, since there always seems to be *someone* crashing—usually a musician. I once spent three months down the hall from David Drake, the bassist from the Kungfu Cowboys. He had a nervous breakdown and spent the entire summer building model airplanes in one of our guest rooms. Whatever.

Our house is on the Hudson River in Nyack, New York. Kind of trendy. A perky talk-show host who never ceases gabbing about her children on the air lives next door. Guess what? The kids are raised entirely by nannies. I'm surprised Ms. Perky Talk-show Host even knows their names. But we can barely see their house through the big pines that surround our property. Our house is pretty, with an immense back lawn that touches the water. I live on the third floor, in what used to be the attic. My parents finished it off so I now have my own living room and bedroom. And that means no more sharing the bathroom with musician houseguests.

I shut the car door and started to head up to the front porch. Toby cleared his throat. "Liv?"

I turned around. Toby weighs a good 280—all muscle— and he shaves his head, but he has this enormous handle-bar mustache that curls around his mouth and makes him look like some kind of weird Kewpie doll.

"Yeah?"

"He's trying."

"I know."

"Cut him some slack. He's going to need a lot of support on this tour." I nodded. Toby was in AA too, but unlike Dad, Toby had been sober for twenty years or something like that. My father pretty much fell off the wagon about every six months. Now he had nearly a year under his belt. I hoped he could stay out of trouble on the tour—no women, no drugs, no alcohol. The last tour ended with him in rehab. The tour before that with two nights in jail.

"I know, Toby. We're all worried." I turned and climbed up the steps and into the house, and then kept on going—all the way up to my room. When I was little, in my mind I used to pretend Toby was my father.

When I got upstairs I turned on my stereo and popped a CD in—one I burned myself. I make a CD every week of all my favorites. That changes from day to day, song to song. Sometimes I can get into a "phase"—like only Nine Inch Nails for a week—usually when I have PMS. Sometimes I hear an old song—from my parents' generation, like the Rolling Stones' "Sympathy for the Devil," or music from the Seattle grunge era—and I can literally listen to the same song two hundred times. It's in me, part of me. I put on my current set of favorites and started jumping up and down on my bed, thinking about the assignment I had just scored. *Holy shit! I got it! I got it!* Rock On!

I called Cammie, my best friend, who had begged for two whole weeks and talked her parents into letting her go on tour with us for the summer. They thought it would be a great opportunity for her to see the world. I wasn't sure what they thought of my father's reputation, but I also knew they were so close to a divorce that maybe it didn't matter—just having Cammie away while they tried to work things out would be good. They were letting her older brother live in Boston that summer. He's going to college there. Anyway, her father could never say no to her. She had him twisted around her little pinkie.

"I got it, Cam!" I screamed into my cell phone. I had stopped jumping and flopped straight backward down on my bed. For some weird reason, I love doing that—except for the one time I hit my head on the wall and had to get stitches.

"Oh, my God! That's *so* awesome!"

"They're even *paying* me."

"Wow! Money is good. Next thing you know, you'll have your own reality show. Paul James's daughter as rockstar critic. You could call it *Livy's Real World*."

"No, I think my life has enough reality it in already."

"I'm so happy for you."

"I can't believe it. My name in print . . . in a real magazine."

"You'll get into NYU's journalism program for sure."

For as long as I can remember, Cammie and I have been planning to go to New York University together. She has always wanted to study filmmaking. She used to wander around with a camcorder all the time. We have visions of sharing an apartment in Greenwich Village.

"You excited?" I asked her. We'd been planning this summer tour together as soon as the Babydolls announced their concert dates.

"Two days and counting!" She sounded like she was hyperventilating.

"I know. I am so psyched. And remember, Cam, *one* suitcase. You can't get nuts." I was picturing clothes from one end of her room to the other.

"I know. One *big* suitcase."

"Yes, one big suitcase and one carry-on. But it's not like the suitcase can be the size of your closet, so I don't know how you're whittling down all your crap into one bag."

"I'll manage."

Cammie was a major clotheshorse. Juicy Couture and Abercrombie & Fitch—her two favorites. What she didn't have, she borrowed—from me. She was also a makeup nut, and I think she had no less than fifty-two kinds of shampoo in her bathroom. I kind of liked sleeping over at her house because I felt like I was at a spa—getting to pick shampoos, conditioners, soaps, cleansers. You can't see her bathroom counter, it's so full of stuff.

"Anything new on Operation V?" she asked me.

"I refuse to help you anymore."

"Oh, come on."

Cammie was determined to lose her virginity—in a scheme that made our history teacher's description of the landing at Normandy in World War II sound like a casual battle plan.

"All right. I just found out this morning that Steve Zane is not bringing anyone on the tour."

"No one?"

"Nope. His latest girlfriend left him."

"Operation V going according to plan."

Cammie intended to lose her virginity to the bassist of the Babydolls. He's younger than my dad by maybe ten years, and he's a total slut. But Cammie had a theory about losing her virginity.

"Are you *sure* you want to go through with this, Cam?"

"Absolutely. As I have said a thousand times before, I have yet to meet a single person who ranked their virginity-losing partner as anyone great. I mean, sure, you think you're in love with some hot guy and you lose your virginity to him. Twenty years from now, he's just some dumb

12

guy you lost your virginity to. Most people are lucky if they remember the guy's name. But if I lose *my* virginity to Steve Zane, even when you and I are ninety and have false teeth and side-by-side rocking chairs in the nursing home, I'll remember exactly who it was—and to top it off, he's probably quite good at it."

"Whatever, Cam. Just don't say I didn't warn you. Every nanny I ever had in my life quit because he'd sleep with her and then dump her a week later in a different city. They'd all go home crushed."

"But *I* know exactly what I'm doing. I'm losing my virginity for historical reasons. I can tell my *grandchildren* that I did it with Steve Zane."

"Yeah. I often discuss sex with my grandmother."

"Well, you get the idea. This isn't about a relationship. It's a quest. It's the Holy Grail of Virginity. You can't tell me you don't think Steve Zane is totally fucking hot."

I admit it. He is. Brown hair, blue eyes, really full lips, high cheekbones. He was the Babydoll the magazines said was "the pretty one."

"Cammie, you know my rule."

"Yes." She sighed. "Livy James's first rule of the opposite sex: No musicians need apply."

"Trust me, Cam. After a few weeks on the road, you'll never look at a band the same way again."

Sex, drugs, and rock and roll.

It's not always all it's cracked up to be.

But then again, it's the only life I've ever known.

Chapter Two

"Crimes of Paris"
—Elvis Costello

TO: Carl Erikson
CC: Rob Hernandez
FR: Livy James
RE: Start of Babydolls article

The Babydolls were done in by big hair and Aqua Net. Don't let the metalheads fool you. Yes, Tommy Lee and Nikki Sixx were running through groupies like you and I run through toilet paper, but they were still putting on makeup and using ungodly amounts of hair spray. And this brought down the Babydolls.

The influential supergroup wasn't as trendy as New Wave, though they influenced that period of music. And they weren't as bad-boy-rock-and-roll as the Rolling Stones—almost, but not quite. They were writing thoughtful lyrics in an era of hair bands. The big-haired guys had song titles like "Teaser," "Glitter," and "Baby Gets Around." The Babydolls wrote about pain, angst, and, in one song, an existential crisis.

But maybe it wasn't Aqua Net that did them in. Not really. It wasn't until a crazed night in

Paris that the Babydolls really ended. In Paris, in a drug- and alcohol-fueled hotel room–destroying binge, Greg Essex and Paul James—best friends until Paul married Greg's ex-girlfriend—finally had it out. As band lore has it, Greg pulled out a gun, aimed it at Paul, and shot a lamp, and Paul charged him, trying to throw him off the balcony. After hotel security and their own bodyguards broke it up, the two bandmates didn't lay eyes on each other for five long years. Now my father, Paul James, is going to spend two months with the man who once tried to kill him.

And the rest of us—the quasi-family of Baby-doll friends and children and lovers? We're just holding our collective breath and praying they don't kill each other.

Chapter Three

"Lifestyles of the Rich and Famous"
                              —Good Charlotte

"Oh, my friggin' God, will you look at that?"

Cammie was running from window to window looking out at the city of Tokyo, then dashing into our bathroom—which was so big her voice echoed—and checking out the little soaps.

"This tub is huge. I could swim in it!" she called out, standing *in* the empty tub. I was still looking at the view.

Japan is surreal. It's as if the inventor of neon, after a three-day bender marked by mass consumption of coffee, decided to create a city just to show off his stuff. Everywhere you look in Tokyo, you see lights. And they dance and move and demand that your senses go into overdrive. You don't know where to look because there's just too much of it. Too many signs, buildings, neon lights, and even people—masses of people with black hair as far as the eye can see. Cammie, with her long blond hair, was suddenly like a movie star as we had walked into our hotel—she was a magnet for men. Mostly she wanted to be a magnet for Steve Zane.

"Does he know how old I am?" she yelled out from the bathroom.

I started to unpack. We had three nights scheduled in Tokyo. We were staying at the Asaka Prince Hotel, and the

Babydolls and the Wolves had the top two floors, though the Wolves weren't scheduled to arrive for another four hours. We had 180-degree views of the city—lit up in its glory—and in the distance, the snowy-topped Mount Fuji, which was hard to make out at night.

"Well, he'd have to be an idiot not to know how old you are. Everyone in the band knows how old *I* am. You're my best friend. Stands to reason he'd know we're both about to start our senior year."

"That could work in my favor." She finally emerged from the bathroom and was now looking through the mini-bar.

I had been on the road with my parents so many times, I knew the art of packing lightly. As my mother used to tell me, that was what hotel dry-cleaning service was for. I finished in two minutes, turned down the bedspread, and flopped onto my bed. The expensive sheets felt smooth against my skin.

"Work in your favor how?"

"I mean it, Livy. You know, the whole hot-schoolgirl thing."

"Sure, Cam. You can prance around backstage like Britney Spears in her 'Oops! . . . I Did It Again' video. Or was that 'Baby One More Time'? Back when she was kind of sexy and hadn't yet crossed over into skanky territory."

Cammie threw a sweater at me. "Shut up. Or I just might." She began doing this mocking Britney impersonation.

I laughed. "You need kneesocks and a schoolgirl uniform."

She went to her bed and grabbed a pillow and threw it at me. It landed on my face.

"Liv?"

"Hmm?" I yawned, taking the pillow off my head. I was achy. Major jet lag.

"What's with your mom? She seems all bummed out. I mean . . . we flew here on a private jet. They were serving champagne and fresh strawberries and sushi. You could turn your seat into a *bed*. They had personal DVD players—very cool, by the way. And she had on those big shades, and she wouldn't talk to anyone."

"My mother hates Greg. She hates the Babydolls. She hates George, their manager, especially."

"Is that the one you call the Vampire?"

I nodded. "Yeah, and she hates the whole idea of the tour."

"Why'd she come?"

"Trust me. She'd rather be home in New York. She'd like nothing better than to garden at our house and spend every weekend out at our beach house, but everyone knows my father can't even match his socks without her. She's here to keep my father out of trouble. She was there the night Greg fired the gun at him—thank God he was too fucked up to actually *aim*. But she just thinks this whole thing is asking for trouble."

"So why's your dad doing it?"

"Millions of dollars. Ever since that movie came out that featured that Babydolls song, they've been hot again. It's like they won the lottery. The record company is just waving truckloads of cash at them. And you can't watch the TV for five minutes without catching that American Express commercial. God, they're making so much money off of this reunion tour, they felt like they couldn't turn it down."

"I wish I had that problem."

"And, on top of all that money, in case you haven't noticed, my father is a fame junkie. You know how he loves to attract attention. I mean, all these years he could have cut his hair, blended in. But he loves being *Paul James,* rock god. King of the microphone and the tight jeans. But my mother and I just hope he can keep his act together."

"Toby will keep him straight."

I shook my head. "Toby can only do so much. I mean, he can babysit my father, but in the end, Dad is the one who has to stay clean. Mom can't do it for him either, so she gets upset. I don't pay too much attention to it all. My parents' soap opera has been going on as long as I can remember. If we can get through the summer with no overdoses, no unexpected pregnancies, no orgies, no one falling off the wagon—and no gunshots—it'll be a miracle."

"My parents' most dramatic moment was when my father made an ass of himself at his law firm's Christmas party."

"Consider yourself lucky."

"I don't. However, I *used* to think you were the luckiest girl I knew. I mean, look at this hotel room all to ourselves. However, truthfully, I'm not so sure you're all that lucky. Father with lamp shade on head versus parents with orgy in the living room? It's a wonder you're not in therapy."

"They used to send me. Then Dr. Cashman wised up and figured out *they* were the ones who needed head-shrinking, not me. I do owe him for one thing, though."

"What?"

"Dr. Cashman was the one who got me into writing. He kept telling me to put my feelings down on paper. When I was done writing feelings, I started writing about what I loved: music."

"And now you're going to be in *Rock On*. I can just imagine the look on that bitchy Susan 'My Shit Don't Stink' Bell's face when she sees you in there. She reads that magazine religiously, you know."

"I know." I smirked. "That's almost the best part about it."

"So, what do you want to do tonight?"

"I'm so tired, Cam."

"We have to do something. It's our first night on the tour. You're used to the high life. Me? I plan on going out every chance we get."

"All right. What do *you* want to do?"

"Go out for sushi and karaoke?" I groaned. "No karaoke. I beg you."

"Oh, come on. No one knows us here. Even if they run shrieking from the room at the sound of your voice, we'll be in London in a week and no one will remember."

Cammie loves to sing. I, on the other hand, may have inherited my father's blue eyes and my mother's thick black hair—but I did not inherit either of their musical talent. Not that I don't love music. My iPod mini's right at its thousand-song limit. I live to write about music, listen to music. It's the soundtrack to my life. But I can't sing. Or play guitar. I can pick out "Mary Had a Little Lamb" on the baby grand piano in our living room. And I can bang a tambourine like the musically challenged Carl "I Wanna Be a Rock Star" Erikson. But that's the extent of it.

"Sushi, maybe. But no karaoke."

"Great. Slimy eel but no singing. Only Livy would look at it that way. Can we drink sake? What's the drinking age here?"

I shrugged. "I don't know. We both look older anyway." I leaned up on one elbow. "Pass me a water bottle from the minibar. I'm so dry from the flight."

Cammie handed me a water, and I drank it while watching her pull out all her outfits. I had never seen someone cram so much stuff into one suitcase.

"If you buy anything on the tour, Cam, you'll have to ship it home. I don't think you could fit a friggin' Tic Tac in your suitcase."

"My father had to sit on it to close it."

"We'll have to commandeer Toby as chief suitcase sitter."

She finished unpacking; then we both showered and changed. She put on her little Juicy Couture pants and top—in pink, with JUICY spelled out on her ass. I wore my usual jeans and a retro rock-and-roll T-shirt. I shop a lot in thrift stores down in Greenwich Village, and then my mom adds rhinestones and things to whatever I buy so my outfits are totally hot and very different. People ask me all the time where I get them. I keep telling Mom to start a business, but she never will.

21

Cammie and I took the elevator to the restaurant. One bank of wall was all windows. The night sky was lit up like a fireworks show of neon. I was tired—but in a jet-lag-tired kind of way. I knew if I lay down I would be like Scarlett Johansson's character in *Lost in Translation.* I'd be staring at Japanese TV until four o'clock in the morning. Better to stay up later and then try to crash hard.

People were lined up on high stools at the sushi bar, and two American men were singing a bad karaoke version of "Back in the USSR" by the Beatles.

The hostess told us that if we waited, she could get us a table. So we listened to *bad* karaoke. Several Japanese men sang in both Japanese and English. An Australian with *way* too much sake to his credit did an Elvis song, and finally Cammie and I got a round table by the windows.

"I love this," Cammie said.

"What? The bad singing?"

"No, we're in *Tokyo,* Livy. Yesterday we were in our boring old lives, and today we're in Japan. And we just sign for everything and stay in a beautiful hotel in a city that's so different. I don't know if this life is a fair trade-off for the time your father drove his Mercedes through the pizzeria, but it's very cool."

"You think it's really cool now. Talk to me in eight weeks, when every hotel room starts to look the same and you miss your mother's spaghetti and meatballs."

"I won't miss them that much, believe me. Meatballs versus this view? I'll take the view."

When our waitress came over, Cammie ordered us two

sakes. The waitress didn't blink and didn't ask for ID. Then we ordered some sushi rolls and sashimi. When the hot sake came with the little sake cups, we toasted each other and the tour.

Another hot sake later, Cammie was singing a Beyoncé tune while men stared at her. I was used to that. We've been best friends since eighth grade, and she's never treated me differently because of who my father is. I live for Mrs. Wilson's meatballs, while Cammie lives for the five pinball machines in our game room. I like that her father doesn't get drunk and fall face-first into his dinner; she likes that my parents apparently don't know what the word *curfew* means. I consider it a fair trade-off. Besides, Mrs. Wilson's meatballs are *that* good.

When Cammie finished her song (complete with one of those Beyoncé ass shakings), everyone applauded. She took a bow like the semidiva she is, then came back over to me.

"I'm having so much fun."

We sat there talking and laughing until the restaurant started to get empty. Around twelve thirty in the morning, Japanese time, I looked up from my little sake cup.

"Cam . . ." I whispered. "There's Nick Hoffman and Kai Logan from the Wolves. Don't be obvious."

They looked confused and tired. Jet-lagged. Which I guess was how Cam and I looked—with three sakes to our credit, though her lip gloss was still perfect—and I'm not sure how she does that. She swears it's because she doesn't let a morsel of food actually *touch* her lips. I think she made a pact with the devil.

23

She glanced over, acting very casual. "Have you met them before?"

I shook my head. "No, but I guess since we're all on the tour we should introduce ourselves. I kind of feel like a dork. But if they see us tonight, and then see us backstage, we'll look like idiots tomorrow. Besides, I need to get an interview with them."

"God, he's even better looking in person. How is that possible?"

"Who?"

"Don't give me that bullshit. You know exactly who. And *you* get to take his picture."

Nick Hoffman shaved his blond hair very close to the scalp, and his face was as angular as a model's. He spoke with an Irish accent—just a hint of a brogue. He'd been raised in England as well as Ireland. Blue-gray eyes, which looked green in his videos sometimes. He seemed to always have a perpetual sexy stubble. I never knew whether that was for the benefit of video and photo shoots, or if he was just too lazy to shave very much.

His bandmate, Kai, most often went by a one-name moniker—like Madonna, Bono, Usher, Sting, and Beyoncé. His mother was Japanese, and his father was British. I knew all this from reading about them in different articles. The band was also politically active, so a portion of the proceeds from every Wolves concert went to a nature conservancy that bought up rain-forest land for preservation.

"Come on," I said to Cammie, and we stood up and approached them.

"Hi." I stuck out my hand. "I'm Livy James, Paul James's daughter."

"Great. A friendly face in Japan." Nick Hoffman smiled at me. "I'm Nick. This is Kai."

"I'm Cammie, Liv's best friend." She smiled and offered her hand.

"You eaten yet?" Nick asked us.

I nodded.

"Just listening to the music then?"

"That and drinking sake."

"Can we join you for a spell?"

"Sure."

The four of us sat down, and Kai didn't look at the menu. When the waitress came he ordered what sounded like an ungodly amount of sushi in Japanese.

"You excited about the tour?" I asked them both.

Kai shrugged. "Yeah. It's good for the album, but after a while you get so wrecked on tour—so tired."

Nick nodded. "It gets old, you know. It's all right now. When we've been on the road so long we don't know what time zone we're in, it can get brutal."

I nodded.

"And for us," Nick continued, "it's also radio show after radio show, television. You know, it's not just being on the stage. We have to talk to magazines that are just fookin' rubbish. Trash. Like *Rock On*. Total piss."

Cammie's eyes widened. She stared at me. Then Nick.

"What? I'm sorry . . . sorry. Ol' pub mouth comes out when I'm shattered—um, tired to you Americans. I shouldn't talk like that."

"It's not that," Cammie said, looking at me again.

"What then? You *like* that magazine?"

"No. It's crap," I said. "Total crap. But I write for it. I'm covering the tour."

Kai looked over at Nick.

"Very smooth, pretty boy. Let's see you talk your way out of this one."

Chapter Four

"See?" Nick smiled. "This is what happens when I try to talk to a beautiful girl when I have jet lag. Just tell me to shove off, okay?"

"Fine." I winked at him. "Shove off."

He laughed. "Now let me get this straight. I thought you said you were Livy James."

"I am."

"But you write for *Rock On?*"

Cammie nodded. "For the summer. She's supposed to write about what it's like on the road."

Nick shook his head. "What a fookin' arsehole I am. I'm sorry for what I said about your magazine."

"It's all right. I kind of think it's crap, too. But I'm a good writer. And you can make it up to me by letting me interview you."

If I had been home—if I had been anywhere else—I never would have been able to say that. But sake and jet lag, and the fact that he was so damn hot . . . well, I just blurted it out and hoped I wasn't blushing.

"Fine. Tomorrow. On one condition."

"What?"

"I pick the time and place."

"Okay. Where and when?"

His eyes twinkled. "Now, now, lass, you don't get to know that. That's my secret."

The waitress came over with a huge sushi boat, which she set down on our table.

Kai looked at Cammie. "Want some? I ordered enough for all of us."

"Oh, that was nice of you, but like we said, we already ate."

"Come on. Bet you didn't have this." He pointed with his chopsticks to a piece of sushi that frankly resembled a greasy tire coated with sauce on rice.

"You're right; we didn't." Cammie winced. But she's never one to back down. She put out her chopsticks and took the "tire sushi" and ate it in one bite. She looked like one of those people on *Fear Factor*. Kai seemed to be delighting in the fact that her mouth twisted like she'd just eaten a live cockroach.

"Wanna know what it is?"

She shook her head and swallowed, then tossed back a cup of sake. "Not really. God, I think it slithered down my throat. I think it was still alive."

"Brave girl." Kai grinned at her.

"You need to tell him to lay off. He does this shit to me all the time," Nick said. "I never ate sushi until I met this wanker."

Karaoke had stopped, and now a piano player at a baby grand was softly playing some vaguely jazz-sounding tune.

"So, Livy . . . you along for the whole tour?" Nick asked.

I nodded. "Both of us."

"Great." Kai smiled. I could tell he liked Cammie.

28

"You must be used to all this by now," Nick said.

I shrugged. "Kind of."

"I think your old man is cool."

"You could say that." You could also say he was a pain in my ass.

"I grew up listening to the Babydolls, and to tour with them . . . it's unreal."

Out of the corner of my eye, I spotted the hostess and a small cluster of people excitedly gathered near the entrance to the restaurant. It could only be one of the Babydolls; I just couldn't see who. If you weren't a rabid Wolves fan, Kai and Nick looked like two good-looking guys in slightly cooler-than-normal clothes. But the Babydolls—even if you weren't a die-hard fan—had been around long enough to seep into the celebrity unconscious. Most people recognized them. They'd done commercials, been on *Saturday Night Live,* toured the globe a few times over, and been on MTV almost as long as MTV had been around.

I suddenly felt myself being the recipient of a sharp kick to the shin.

"Ouch." I gave Cam a dirty look.

"Livy, it's Steve Zane. We should go say hi to him. Looks like he's here alone."

Despite my aversion to all musicians, the rather playful Nick Hoffman was *far* hotter than anyone I'd ever met. But, aside from that, I thought Cam would be much better off meeting someone like Kai for her Operation V than Steve Zane. I'd seen what he was capable of.

"Why are you crying, Ilsa?"

I was nine, and my au pair, Ilsa, from Sweden, had her face buried in her hands.

"It's nothing, Livy," she said, wiping at her face and then pulling on my pigtails.

"What?"

Her blue eyes were filled with tears. "It's . . . I think I want to go home," she said in an accent that made *think* sound like *zink*.

"Home? We're not going to New York until September," I said.

"No, angel," she said. "I mean *my* home." She smiled through her tears and blew her nose. "You know . . . I tell you all about my home many times."

"Take me with you," I remember saying, clutching her and wrapping my arms around her neck. She always smelled of baby powder.

"I can't, pet."

We were in a hotel in Frankfurt. The door to the hallway was open, and at that moment Steve Zane walked by. Ilsa turned bright red. He didn't even glance at us.

"It's him, isn't it," I whispered after he had passed.

She nodded.

"It's always him. He does this all the time. Don't go home. Please . . . I need you."

Ilsa was beautiful, with long white-blond hair and no need for makeup at all. Her cheeks were naturally rosy, and she was hired because she spoke five languages and was teaching me German and French.

"I have to."

"Don't let him bother you."

"Please understand, Livy. I love you. But . . ." She started crying again.

Ilsa packed that night. She left behind a scarf she knitted for me. I found out later, after my father went to rehab—again—after many things, that Steve had talked her into doing drugs, slept with her, and then kicked her out of his hotel room at three in the morning. He told her he wanted her gone. Off the tour. George, the band's manager, "took care" of things like that. She was offered the band's standard deal: ten thousand dollars to disappear, and a plane ticket home.

She left the next morning. Toby was already my father's bodyguard and driver, and I guess my parents figured he could keep an eye on me if they needed him to. At least he wouldn't be sleeping with the band.

So Toby learned how to make brownies, play Monopoly, and help me with math homework.

And I never had another nanny after that.

I smiled at Cammie. "I'm sure Steve will sit at the sushi bar." In fact, I knew he liked anyplace with a stool far better than a chair. Sushi bar, regular bar—it was all the same to him.

However, Steve surprised me by waving at us and coming over.

"Hey . . . See you guys met each other."

Nick and Kai stood and shook his hand.

"I'm so completely out of whack," Steve said. "Can't sleep."

"Neither can I," Cammie offered. She batted her big blue eyes. God, when she gets an idea in her head, she doesn't think of anything else. It was like the time she was determined to make out with Rory Kilgore—despite the fact that he had come out as gay in the second week of school junior year.

Steve motioned to the sushi chefs. "I'm gonna sit over at the bar. Like watching those guys make the stuff, you know."

"We'll keep you company," Cammie offered.

I wanted to smack her. Just tell her what an ass she was being. Kai looked disappointed, and I can't say Nick looked thrilled. I sighed and stood up.

"Actually, I'm really beat. Jet lag. You stay, Cam." I looked over at Nick. "What time tomorrow?"

"Noon. Lobby. The rest is a surprise."

"Okay." I shrugged. "But I have to tell you, I hate surprises."

"Then obviously the right bloke hasn't been surprising you."

He sure was smooth. I leaned over to shake his hand. Kai stood and kissed me on the cheek. Cammie gave me a hug, and I left the restaurant. I didn't look back. I didn't want Nick Hoffman to think I liked him. Yes, he was cute, but he was a musician. And I didn't want to see what Cammie was doing.

Whatever it was, it was a mistake.

Chapter Five

I wasn't tired. I wasn't even a little bit tired.

I stared at the ceiling. I played my iPod. I put a DVD on my laptop. And in the end, I knew it was a lost cause. I wasn't going to fall asleep, no matter how much sake I'd had—and I'm not much of a drinker anyway. Not after growing up with my father.

When my dad was in rehab, Toby used to drive my mother and me up to Connecticut for "family weekends." Basically, it was group therapy for the people in rehab and the spouses and kids whose lives they'd made a mess of. I don't know that I ever felt sorry for myself. In group therapy, you heard some pretty fucked-up stories. If they could make *my* father and my life sound normal . . . well, then you're talking some serious screwups. And I heard enough stories that I knew I didn't ever want to let myself get in trouble with alcohol or drugs—and maybe more important, besides my no-musicians rule, I had a rule about no heavy drinkers. No one who used drugs regularly.

I looked at the clock and punched my pillow. I thought of Cammie, which made me want to go running out looking for her. I thought of Nick Hoffman and my "surprise" interview tomorrow. I was the journalist here. I thought I

33

was the one in charge. For a few minutes I stared at the ceiling and thought I was in over my head.

I was wearing a big sleep shirt—an extra-extra-large concert T-shirt from the Babydolls "Live from Your Radio" tour. I slipped it over my head and changed into a pair of black yoga pants and a tank, and put on my sneakers. I figured maybe if I went down to the lobby and paced awhile, I might burn off this jet lag and worry and get sleepy.

I left my hotel room and stepped into the absolute silence of the hallway. Everyone was sleeping off the plane trip. I headed down the hall toward the elevators. You needed a special elevator key to even get to our floor—that way no naked groupies could show up to "surprise" anyone in the band. If anyone in either band had a naked groupie in his room, he had brought her there himself.

When I got to the elevator, I heard a door open down the hall. It was Charlie, the Babydolls' drummer.

"Hey, Liv," he said as he approached me. He was wearing a T-shirt and jeans, and he was smoking a cigarette, though there was a no-smoking sign posted in the hallway. He held the cigarette out in front of him. "The one addiction I can't give up."

"What are you doing awake?"

He shrugged. "I never thought about jet lag."

"What do you mean?" We were whispering, though no one could have heard us out in the hallway.

"No pot. No booze. No sleeping pills. I never thought about it, Liv, but that's how I always dealt with jet lag. Now I don't have none of that. And man, I'm climbing the fuckin' walls."

"You've got two years sober, though. Almost three. Hang in there."

He nodded. "Now don't go gettin' all worried about me, Liv. I'm not about to fall off the wagon. Just that I can't sleep."

"Well, neither can I."

"What about Cam?"

"Last I saw her, she was with Steve."

"Oh, man!"

"I know. But she won't listen."

He shook his head. "I forgot about how crazy it could be to live with, eat with, tour with three other guys, their wives, girlfriends, the roadies, and George. Twenty-four/seven. You know, I wish I hadn't blown through so much money. Then I wouldn't need this stupid tour."

He inserted his room key in the elevator lock. "Going down?"

I nodded. "I could use the company. I just want to walk."

"Cool. Come on."

When the elevator doors opened, we stepped inside. We rode down in silence, and I checked out Charlie's reflection in the polished brass of the elevator walls.

He was still hot—for an old guy. He clipped his hair really short compared to when the Babydolls were first together, and it was gray in spots now, but he still looked young, I guess. My mother claims he got a face-lift four years ago. I don't know about that. Then again, he might have had one just to get his hands on pain pills. He had at least nine earrings in each ear, and he wore a goatee. His eyes were dark brown, and it was weird . . . they almost looked like they were lined with eyeliner because they seemed really dark.

The elevator doors opened in the lobby, and several of the front-desk people nodded at us as we left the hotel and made our way out onto the sidewalks of Tokyo. Like in New York City, people were still out, and cars still zoomed by even at two in the morning.

I thought of how Carl wanted me to look at the history of the Babydolls. So I decided this was my chance to see what Charlie thought about the band, my father, the life they'd lived together.

"Charlie?"

"Yeah, baby?" They all called me that. He took a last drag off his cigarette and tossed it in the gutter. The streets were so clean, I thought maybe he shouldn't have, but all of the Babydolls—in fact every musician I'd ever met— were overgrown children. They were used to being worshiped, and that meant they didn't have to follow the rules made for everyone else. My father, for instance, always cuts to the front of any line. And 99 percent of the time he gets away with it, because people are starstruck.

"What do you remember about when the band started?"

"What? When I met your father and Greg?"

I nodded. We had fallen in sync with each other, strolling. I kept looking around at the buildings and neon. I've always found it strange to be in a foreign country. It's isolating if you don't speak the language. You feel very alone because you can't communicate with anyone, so walking in the night with Charlie made me feel as if we were the only two people in all of Japan.

"Well," he said, "back then, Livy, we made music because we loved it. At least I did. I heard Charlie Watts from
the Stones on 'Honky-Tonk Woman,' I think. I don't know.
I remember hearing the drums, and I just knew I wanted to
make music. Your dad and Greg and I never thought we'd
have a hit record. Hell, that was when there *were* records
and not CDs. We didn't care about being famous. We cared
about the songs. The guys were my best friends. We
hooked up with Steve. He was a real kid—not even legal,
dropped out of high school. And we all just had fun. I
mean, it was a blast at first. I never had so many laughs in
my life."

"Is it still fun?"

He thought about it for a minute.

"No. Then it all turned to shit. It all got crazy, Liv. Now
it's a job. It's how I pay for Jack to go to college. It's how I
pay for private school for Elizabeth. It's how I pay alimony
to three ex-wives. It's a gig, Liv."

"When did it all get so screwed up?"

"Well, I suppose it was when we had our second single
go to number one. Me . . . I'm an okay-looking guy, but no
one gives a crap about the drummer. I mean, yeah, the
drummer is cool and all, but your father and Greg . . . the
girls went wild over them. Suddenly we went from playing
midsize clubs and places like CBGBs in New York to playing Madison motherfucking Square Garden."

"Is that what they call it?"

He gently gave my shoulder a little push. "You've become quite a little wiseass, Liv. I remember when you used

to come on tour and all you wanted to do was write in that diary of yours and read books. You were so quiet."

"I was just trying to keep out of the way. Keep out of the craziness."

"Yeah. I mean, we reached a point where we were like a hurricane. We just destroyed everything in our path—hotel rooms, our own bodies with drugs and an ocean of alcohol, our marriages, our children. I went from being just this guy in a band, to this guy who couldn't go out in public without a baseball cap and sunglasses on. They don't tell you how to deal with that."

"What? You mean it's not in the *How to Be a Rock Star* handbook?"

He laughed. "Exactly. We weren't ready for fame. I don't think anyone ever is. Not for that level of it. No one tells you what a rush it is to listen to a hundred thousand people screaming for you to come on stage. To have people name their children after you, to have them tattoo the Babydolls' logo on their ass."

"So is this tour just for the money?"

"Yes and no. It's for closure. Things after that night in Paris got so crazy, and then we didn't speak for the longest time. But Livy, there are only three other people in the whole of the universe who know what it's like to be a Babydoll. So I'm here, on this tour, to kind of make peace with it all. It's bigger than I am—bigger than all of us—and I need to make peace with it. And I've got a money manager now—a really smart guy—so I'm taking all the money I'm making from this and investing it, and then I'm going to retire to Woodstock, New York. I've got the farm up there, you know. Remember going up with me and my wife at the time one weekend with your folks?"

I nodded. I remembered he had horses. "Hey, can I ask you something?"

"Haven't you already?" He smiled at me.

"Why did you get sober finally?"

Charlie stopped in the middle of the sidewalk and turned to face me. He took a deep breath, looked away, then looked back at me.

"My doctor told me if I didn't lay off the booze, I wouldn't live to see my fiftieth birthday. Which was totally all right with me. My motto was, 'Live fast, die young, and leave a pretty corpse.' Until I realized that I loved Jack and Elizabeth. Even if I was a pretty shitty father, I was the only one they had. And I loved Elizabeth's mother."

"Serena?"

He nodded. "I decided I had something to live for. That this whole crazy life had been about me running away from the people I loved. I figured it out finally, but Serena left me anyway. I'd messed up a whole lot. But I got sober for my kids."

"You still love Serena?"

He nodded.

"Have you ever told her how you feel?"

He shook his head.

"Well, you should. You should try to win her back."

"Maybe."

"Come on, let's go back to the hotel. And you send her an e-mail . . . or call her."

"I'll think about it."

We walked back to the hotel. I still wasn't sure if I could sleep. When we got up to our floor, I kissed Charlie on the cheek.

"You and my dad . . . hang tight. Don't drink. No matter what Steve and Greg are doing."

He nodded and turned and walked alone down the hall to his room.

I opened the door to Cam's and my room. She was sitting up in her pajamas.

"He kissed me!" she squealed.

"And?"

"Nothing else. But he said I was different."

"And you believe him?"

"Oh, don't be mad, Liv. He's soooo cute."

"So's Kai."

"He's not my type."

"What? Nice guys aren't your type?"

"Well, there's something very hot about Steve."

I got undressed and put my sleep shirt on again. "I'm beat. Let's just get some sleep."

Cammie looked hurt and crawled under the covers and turned her back toward me.

I climbed into my bed and turned off the lamp. But I can't stay mad at Cam. In the darkness, I said, "So was he a good kisser?"

"The absolute best, Livy. The absolute best."

Chapter Six

"Family Reunion"
—Blink 182

The next day, Cammie and I slept in until eleven o'clock Tokyo time, which left me exactly one hour to get ready to meet Nick Hoffman.

"Cam, are you *sure* you don't mind?"

"Positive. Personally, I think it's romantic."

"There's no romance, Cam."

"Whatever you say."

"I mean it. Yes, he's hot, but I wouldn't hook up with a musician if he was the last man on earth. Look, he has so many girls screaming for him in every city. I've seen enough of that life up close with my father. No way, Cam. Not a chance."

"Sure. Why have Nick Hoffman when you can have one of the dorks or freaks from our high school?" She rolled over and stretched. She woke up looking perfect. I could almost hate her if she weren't my best friend.

"Shut up. I've got to get moving or I'll be late. What are you going to do today?" I didn't want her to feel like I was abandoning her in the middle of Tokyo.

"I want to go shopping. Think Toby will take me?"

"I'll ask. I can't imagine that he wouldn't. Let me go down to my parents' suite and see."

I took a fast shower and pulled on jeans, a pair of black

41

boots, and one of the rock T-shirts my mom made me—this one from an old Talking Heads concert. Yes, I love Eminem and hip-hop and new stuff, but I really love the old stuff, too. It depends on whether I want to dance, have a good cry, rock out and scream at the top of my lungs, or just hang out. That's the best part of music—it's for every mood.

I went down to the very far end of the hall and knocked on my parents' door. I didn't expect them to be up, but my mom appeared in a green silk robe, sipping a cup of herbal tea.

"You're up early," she said to me. "I would have thought you and Cammie would sleep until supper."

"I have an interview today with Nick Hoffman. In . . ." I looked at my watch. ". . . about forty minutes."

"Be careful." She sat down at the large dining room table—it was a huge suite. Fresh flowers filled every corner. It was so big, it was almost like an apartment. I could hear my father singing in the shower. Cam says her father sings Frank Sinatra once in a while. My father sings the Clash.

"Be careful of what?"

My mother waved her hand. "Nothing." She still wore her hair long, to the middle of her back, the way my dad likes it, and it was still very dark, almost black—she didn't have to dye it like Cammie's mom. My mother looks thirty-five. She's older than that, in her forties, but she dresses like any of the other girlfriends on the tour—jeans and tight T-shirts, heels. She never goes out in the sun without a hat or sunscreen on, so no wrinkles. She's really beautiful. She says she has to stay in shape—has to stay young looking—because my father's a rock star. It means he's a magnet for women.

"What, Mom? What do you mean, 'Be careful'? You can't just say something like that, then drop it."

"All right, then. Be careful of Nick Hoffman."

I shook my head. "Why? You don't even know him, Mom."

"Livy, you're seventeen, and I know you think you know everything, because you're very smart and a very good writer and you're going to go to college—which neither your father nor I did. But you don't know everything. Some things you can only learn from experience. I just don't want to see you get hurt."

"Mom . . . it's an *interview,* not a date."

"I know, but just be careful. He and the rest of the Wolves are just a couple of years older than you and Cammie, and I'm responsible for Cammie on this tour. And I also don't want to see you—or her—trailing after some singer or musician like two puppy dogs."

"Jeez, Mom! You have a lot of nerve. First of all, I'm *nothing* like you. Nothing. I'm not stupid, Mom. This is my job, to cover the tour, and it's what'll get me into NYU. It'll look great on my college application . . . and . . . Just forget it. You didn't even sound that excited when I told you about the job. Dad was excited, but you weren't."

"Livy." She stood up and came over to me to try to give me a hug.

I stepped away. "You know, Mom, just because you and Dad messed up your lives doesn't mean I'm going to."

With that, my father stepped naked out into the hotel room. "Oh, man!" he shouted, and went back for a towel. He came out again. "What's going on?"

My mother sighed. "As usual, she takes after you—stubborn."

I turned to my mother. "I don't take after either of you. And I don't need your advice. I can take care of myself. If I want to ask someone for advice, I'll go to Toby." I turned and stormed out of their room. I could hear my father calling out, "Livy," from behind the door as I slammed it.

I looked at my watch. "Ugh!" I ran down the hall to Toby's room and knocked quietly. He opened the door immediately.

"Morning," he said. He was in gym shorts and a tank. For not the first time, I was amazed at his body. He has muscles on *top* of muscles.

"Sorry to bother you," I said. I could see a treadmill in the middle of his room and some free weights. The benefits of touring with a rock band: You can demand anything from weights and treadmills to only green M&M's in the candy bowl backstage. The Babydolls used to insist they be supplied two cases of Jack Daniel's and Coke, fresh fruit and a vegetable platter (my mother is a vegetarian), chicken wings, and peanut M&M's (all colors were okay) in their backstage rooms. I forgot to ask what they wanted this tour.

"No problem, Liv. What's up?" He wiped at his face with a hotel towel.

"I have an interview with Nick Hoffman today. I don't want to leave Cam all alone. Can you take her shopping?"

"Sure. I want to pick up some souvenirs for Lisa anyway."

"You really like her, don't you?"

He nodded. He had met this amazing woman, an artist, at an AA meeting. I had never seen him go crazy over someone before. "She's like my reward for sobriety. I mean, I never could have had a woman like her when I was doing drugs. She's meeting us in L.A. And I've been on the phone with her four times already."

"How cute. Maybe she's the one."

"Maybe." He smiled.

I couldn't imagine what I would do without Toby. I always used to worry he'd meet someone and get married and leave us. But I'm older now, and I guess I finally realized I just wanted him to have someone special. "You should get her a kimono."

"That's what I was thinking. . . . Hey, this is your first big interview."

I smiled. "I know. He was really cool about it, too."

"Can I read it when you're done?"

"Only if you want to, Toby."

"Livy . . . I've been reading your stories since you could hold a pen. Don't you remember when you were, like, ten, and you wrote that story about the rock-and-roll mice? You know, who played like a Mouse Woodstock?"

"Oh, God, yeah. Well, hopefully I've improved."

"I'm not going to know what to do with myself when you go off to NYU."

"I have a feeling my father will keep you busy enough. . . . But I'll miss you, too. You're the only sane one. I just got in a fight with Mom."

"Over what?"

"The interview. She thinks I'm going to fall for Nick

Hoffman and make the same stupid mistakes she did. Well, I'm not a groupie. And I never will be."

Toby smiled and stepped forward and hugged me. "Any man who mistook Livy James for a groupie wouldn't live long enough to tell about it. I'll talk to your mom. Now you get outta here. You got your big interview. Knock 'em dead. . . . Oh, and tell Cammie to come find me when she's ready. And maybe I can talk some sense into her about Steve Zane. The guy's a lizard."

"Thanks, Toby."

Thirty minutes to go. I ran as fast as I could to my room and raced in, talking at Cam a mile a minute, and went into the bathroom to do my makeup and dry my hair, which was still damp from the shower.

"Toby will take you shopping," I shouted over the blow-dryer. "He wants to pick out a kimono for his new girlfriend. Help him. He's color-blind. I'm not kidding. I actually had to help him pack so he'd have coordinating outfits. Just knock on his door when you're ready. And order whatever you want off of room service for breakfast . . . um, lunch . . . whatever."

Cam came and stood in the doorway to our bathroom.

"Do you know how cool it is to live like this? I mean, people like Madonna live like this. I'm going to have to become a really famous filmmaker, and you're going to have to become a huge journalist so we can keep up this lifestyle when we're older."

I bent over at my waist and aimed the blow-dryer at the roots of my hair, then flipped back up, turned it off, and started putting on mascara, eyeliner, and lip gloss.

46

"It is cool. Room service is my favorite part of the whole thing."

"Room service? I'm talking about shopping in Tokyo. I'm going to run out of money, I just know it."

"We'll sneak some stuff on my credit card. But remember, we're going to be gone eight weeks. So you have a *lot* of shopping to do. Spread it out."

I looked at myself in the mirror. No, I don't have Cammie's all-American-girl looks. My lips are too full—exotic looking is more like it. My eyes sort of look like a cat's. I'm only a B-cup. Well, B and a half. With a Wonderbra, maybe a C. And Cammie and my mother are, like, size one. I wear a four. But the best part about me is my legs. They're like my father's, really long. I used to hate being taller than all the boys in middle school. In high school some of them caught up with me. And now being tall is better. I stand out in a crowd, and people think I'm older than seventeen— which helps when you're trying to get people to take you seriously as a writer.

"You look great, Livy."

"Thanks." I ran to my backpack and dumped its contents on the floor. It was mostly stuff for the plane ride. Gum, candy, a book, my journal. I opened it to the page I started on Nick Hoffman:

Nick Hoffman
Lead singer of the Wolves
Instrument: Can play piano and guitar
Miscellaneous: He's a serious environmentalist, from Ireland, only child, has been best friends with Kai Logan

since his first year of secondary school, supposedly has an IQ of 144, likes soccer and rugby, broke his arm playing rugby before his last tour, now record company has a clause that he can't play within three months of tour dates.

I put my journal back into my knapsack and then scrambled to find my mini tape recorder. "You think he'll let me tape the interview?"

She shrugged. "I don't see why not. Then you're sure to get his quotes right."

I found my tape recorder and put it in the backpack, along with my digital camera. I stuck my lip gloss in there. A pack of gum. A roll of cherry Life Savers.

I stood. "Wish me luck."

"You'll be great."

"Have a good time today. Don't spend all your money. And make sure you're back here by five. Tonight's the first concert."

I dashed out the door and took the elevator down to the lobby. Nick Hoffman was already waiting. He was signing autographs for two little girls. I watched him from across the lobby. The little girls looked American—one had on a Yankees cap, and they were maybe eleven or twelve. He was patient as they jumped up and down with excitement, clearly flustered. He signed the one girl's Yankee cap, and then he put his arms around their shoulders and turned to their mother and father and let them take four or five pictures. He was a lot more gracious than any of the Baby-dolls—who'll sign autographs and take pictures, but get a little crabby about it after all these years of fame. He shook hands with the girls' parents and then let the little girls each give him a peck on the cheek. Then I caught his eye, and he waved to me.

I walked over to him, trying not to feel nervous.

"Ready?" He looked very mischievous.

"I think so."

"Come on then." He grabbed my hand and led me outside through the immense lobby doors. There, sitting on the sidewalk, stood a red Vespa. Two helmets sat on the seat.

"You can't be serious," I said.

"Deadly serious. It's the only way to see Tokyo."

Chapter Seven

"Karma Police"
—Radiohead

I looked at him. "I don't know how to drive one of these."

"But I do. Come on." He handed me a helmet.

"How can I do an interview with this on my head? I won't be able to talk to you."

"But we're going someplace where we can talk all afternoon."

"Where?"

"Come on. I told you. A surprise. Where's your sense of adventure, lass?"

I looked down at the helmet. So much for blow-drying my hair. I'd have helmet head in under five minutes. I shrugged and put it on. Real journalists sometimes do stuff with the people they interview. I'd just have to go with it.

Nick Hoffman stepped over the motorcycle and moved forward so there was room for me to sit in back of him. I climbed on. It felt weird, considering he was basically a stranger, but I clasped my hands around the front of him and slid up close. His stomach was rock hard. And he smelled really good.

"Ready?"

"Yeah. I guess."

He started up the Vespa and eased into the crowded streets of Tokyo. We zipped between cars—good thing I don't panic easily—and zoomed on through the city. In the light of day, Tokyo was still a place of strange sights and sounds. Neon still glowed—though fainter in the sunlight—and it was busy. I had never seen so many people in my life—not even in Manhattan. The buildings were tall and gleamed with glass in the noonday sun. Overlooking it all was Mount Fuji in the distance, like a wise goddess guarding the gates of paradise. Clouds clustered around the peak, so you couldn't see the very top.

"Beautiful, huh?" Nick nodded in the mountain's direction, shouting over the engine and traffic.

I nodded and leaned into his shoulder a bit to block the wind hitting my face. I was so conscious of my hands and arms around him. And I didn't have any sake to make me feel less nervous.

Nick steered the Vespa expertly, and eventually the traffic eased enough that I felt less tense, and we were leaving the city limits of Tokyo for God knew where. I leaned back a tiny bit. I could see the hint of a tattoo at the base of his helmet, on the back of his neck. I wondered what it was—it looked like a Chinese symbol.

We drove on, and eventually we seemed to be nearing the mountain. It was still off in the distance, but we were closer to it. Finally he pulled off the main highway and steered us down a wooded road until we stopped in front of a temple. He parked the Vespa, and we both climbed off. My legs still felt like they were shaking from the vibrations of the motorcycle. That and nerves.

He took his helmet off and secured it onto the bike. In the sunlight, I could see his eyes were sort of green. I took my helmet off and handed it to him, and ran my fingers through my hair, hoping my helmet head wasn't completely gross.

"Where are we?"

"Buddhist temple. Come on." We started walking, and I could hear the sound of chanting coming from inside. We entered, and the stone building felt cool inside. I smelled incense. Nick bowed to a statue of the Buddha, clasping his hands together in front of himself, and I did the same, following his lead. I felt disrespectful intruding on the monks, and Nick and I stayed back and watched them, their robes woven with flecks of orange and gold, their voices intoning as one, rising and falling with the words of their prayer. Nick didn't say anything, and we both just listened to their voices. It felt strangely peaceful. Eventually he tapped my arm and nodded for us to leave. We left quietly through a side door and entered a courtyard, and beyond that gardens.

"This place is beautiful," I whispered. Mount Fuji still stood in the distance, as if watching over us. I wished I could see the very top, but the clouds clung to peaks.

He nodded. We walked in silence, and I decided this was the strangest interview experience in the world. Who has a silent interview? I'd have nothing to write. *I walked with Nick Hoffman through a Buddhist temple in silence. The end.* I'd fired for sure. Eventually we found a stone bench that looked as ancient as the temple itself and sat down.

"Why did you bring me here?"

He shrugged. "I was planning on coming anyway, and I thought . . . I don't know . . . that it might be interesting."

"It's quiet," I whispered. "Feels strange even talking in a normal voice. Kind of like church." I opened my backpack and took out my notebook and a pen.

He nodded. "I know *Rock On* does all these . . . well, you said it last night: It's a lot of crap. But I don't feel like I'm terribly interesting, Livy. I mean, really, who cares about whether I like girls with long black hair and blue eyes?" He looked right at me, and I knew I blushed, but brushed my hair forward a bit to hide it.

". . . or blondes, for that matter," he continued. "That's all those magazines talk about. That and what we're like on the road and . . . how 'bout the bloody MTV *Cribs*? I mean, who really cares whether I have a pinball machine in my bathroom and drive a sports car? I don't have either, by the way."

He sighed and looked away. "I feel like I get lost in the whole machine, you know? That's what my song 'The Machine Man' is about."

"Yeah, I know what you mean, a little bit. It never seems to be about the music anymore. And that's why people with no talent can have a number-one hit, and some of the best groups and songwriters can remain obscure. It's all based on whether you want to pay your dues to the machine."

"Exactly. It's about the videos and the look and the bullshit. I mean, you write a song and the first thing people are figuring out is how to shoot a music video to it. And I just thought that maybe if you got to know me you could write a different kind of article. And if not, we'd have a nice day."

"So why here? What can I get to know about you here?"

"I'm a Buddhist, for one thing."

"So that's why we came here."

He nodded.

"What does that symbol on the back of your neck mean?"

He self-consciously moved his hand and rubbed the spot that was tattooed. "Oh, saw that, did you? This . . . it's the Chinese symbol for danger."

"Are you dangerous then?" I flirted with him.

"No. Because it's also the character for opportunity. It's all in how you look at challenges. You can see danger and trouble, or you can accept the danger and learn from it. The Wolves have made it, yeah. But there were four years I lived on nothing but mustard sandwiches."

"How come you're a Buddhist?"

"Karma."

"What do you mean?"

"I mean I believe in doing no harm—to anyone. That what goes around comes around. And I know it's really bull, some actors and musicians just spouting their opinions to hear themselves. You know, whatever comes out of their bloody mouths sounds so self-important. But if I could use my music just a tiny bit as a platform for peace, then that's all right."

I nodded and looked around the gardens. We were the only ones there. "How'd you find this place, anyway?"

"Came here once before. On a vacation, not a tour. It was after we had our first platinum album. I just wanted to go someplace where I didn't know anyone. Or more important, where I didn't think anyone knew me. Shaved my head completely so no one would recognize me. Only got spotted a couple of times. And I got a guide to take me to this temple."

"It's beautiful. Um . . . Can I tape some of this interview?"

"How about I ask you a questions, then you ask me one? If you agree to that, you can tape it."

"This isn't Truth or Dare; it's an interview."

"Well, those are my demands. I'm a spoiled rock star, you know." He looked at me, and his mouth sort of twisted into a smirk. He knew how hot he was. And he knew I needed the story.

"All right." I took out my tape recorder. I scooted back on the bench and put the tape recorder between us. I pressed the record button.

"What does your music mean to you?"

He leaned back against the bench. "It's like breathing. I couldn't live without it. It's all I am . . . . Almost all I am." He paused. "Your turn: What does your writing mean to you?"

I wasn't used to answering questions—not like this. My parents always forbade journalists to ask me questions. I thought for a minute and then said, "It's hard to explain. It's like I'm full of words. They're just bursting in my brain. I wake up with sentences in my mind, and I run to put them down on paper. My brain never shuts off, and for me it's about the words. Your turn. What's your favorite song you ever wrote?"

"I like 'Tuesday at Ten.' It's about that moment . . . you

know . . . when you realize that this person you've just met is going to end up meaning a lot to you. It's about anticipation."

I blushed. This interview felt too intimate. Nick continued, "Your turn: Why does your friend Cammie like that wanker Steve Zane?"

"Excuse me?"

"That was my question. You have to answer it. Rules are rules."

"Do you like Cammie?" I had my no-musicians rule, but my heart still felt like it had swooped down to my stomach.

"Answer the question, please, Ms. James," he teased.

"Fine. Um . . . she likes the challenge more than she actually likes him."

"But he's not really a challenge, is he?"

I shook my head.

"He'll sleep with her if that's what she wants. But Kai really likes her. And not just for a toss in the hay, you know?"

"Oh." I wasn't sure why I felt relieved that he was asking the question for Kai and not himself, but I was. "Your turn: What's the best part of being a rock star? What's the worst?"

"Same answer for both. Fame. It's a kick hearing our songs on the radio. Getting to express myself to an audience. The worst part is the lack of privacy. It's people wanting a piece of you, and they don't even know you or what you're about. It's a girl wanting you just to say she had a toss with one of the Wolves. We did that thing for a while. It don't mean nothing. We figured that out early."

"Some rock stars never figure it out," I said, thinking of Steve and Greg.

"Well, I don't ever want to be someone you read about in the paper—'Rock Star Chokes on Own Vomit' . . . 'One-hit Wonder Dead at Twenty-five.' Whatever. Your turn: What is the best and worst thing about growing up with the Babydolls?"

"I'm not sure there was a best. Maybe being around the music. Oh, and Cammie and I think it's the room service," I joked. "And Toby . . ."

"Who's Toby?"

"Except for Cam, he's my best friend. He's my father's driver, our bodyguard, the guy who wrestles the bottle of Jack Daniel's away from my dad, the one who came to parent-teacher conferences when my parents were off in Europe or wherever."

"Is he on the tour?"

I nodded. "You'll see him. Bald. Handlebar mustache."

"You love him?"

"Not like that. He's just my friend. He's been the one consistent thing in my life—him and music. And the worst? I don't know; I suppose it was seeing my parents all messed up, and watching the people around them act like that was okay. George—their manager—he's like this blood-sucking vampire. Anything they want to do is fine. Trash a hotel room? George will fix it. Get some hot chick to come backstage? He'll take care of that, too. Need to score some drugs? George is your man. I hate him." As I finished talking, I was aware that this interview really wasn't going the way that I wanted it to. "My turn: Who are your biggest musical influences?"

"I don't know . . . we like everyone from the Beatles to the Strokes to Coldplay to Bob Dylan. You can't help but hear things you like in what other people do, but in the end, we make music as the Wolves. It's just us. My turn." He reached down to the tape recorder and turned it off. "Will you have lunch with me tomorrow?"

What was I supposed to do? Tell him my no-musicians rule? It sounded so stupid, so high school, but I had that rule for a reason. I never, ever wanted to get dragged into the band life. It was bad enough to be born into it, but I wasn't going to *choose* a boyfriend in a band. It's just that . . . well, all I could think about was the long ride back to Tokyo, feeling his back pressed against me, my hands around his stomach.

Then, for no reason whatsoever, I heard my mother's voice. *Be careful.* As if she knew anything about my life. I could handle myself. It was only lunch.

"Okay. I guess so."

He smiled and took my face in his hands and kissed my cheek. "Great. Now let's go back to Tokyo."

We stood and walked through the gardens back to the Vespa. I could hear the gurgling of koi ponds, and it was so peaceful compared to the city of neon.

Just before I put my helmet on, I looked up at Mount Fuji. The clouds shifted ever so slightly, and I could glimpse the peak, the top. Maybe it was a good omen. A sign for good luck.

Or maybe I was crazy.

As we rode back to Tokyo, I held Nick tightly. And I kept repeating in my head . . . *It's only lunch.*

It's only lunch.

It's only lunch.

It's only lunch.

If only his abs weren't so sexy.

Chapter Eight

Nick and I rode up in the elevator together. He got off on his floor—one below mine.

"Thanks for the day," I said. "I'm not sure I got enough to write about, but maybe I'll get some quotes tomorrow, too."

Nick's hand leaned up against the door of the elevator so it wouldn't close. "You going to the concert tonight?"

I nodded.

"Good. Pay attention when I sing 'Head in the Clouds.' "

"Okay." I shrugged.

"See you tomorrow. Lobby. Noon. I'm taking you to my favorite restaurant."

"Please tell me it's *in* Tokyo."

"It's a surprise."

With that he let go of the elevator door, and it closed. I rode up one flight to my floor, walked down the hall, and entered my room.

"Cammie?"

I looked around the hotel room. Bags and bags and more bags. Her bed was *covered* in stuff—shirts, skirts, makeup.

Cammie came out of the bathroom wearing what was obviously a new silk kimono—with Hello Kitty on it.

60

"Are you out of your mind?"

"What?"

"Cam, how much did your parents give you for spending money?"

"Two thousand dollars."

"Generous, don't you think?"

"Mmm, yeah, I guess so."

"And how much did you spend today?"

"I'm not really sure. I get confused switching dollars to yen."

"Cam, you've got to return some of this."

"Look, isn't this hot?" She held up a pink miniskirt.

"Adorable. But Cammie . . . you won't have any money left for Paris and London and Germany."

"I'll beg my father for more."

I sighed and rolled my eyes.

"All right. I'll return a few things."

"Good."

"Enough about my little shopping spree. How was your day with Nick?"

"Cam, I don't know. I didn't get nearly enough stuff to write about. He took me on one of those little Vespa motor scooters to a Buddhist temple and gardens. It was beautiful, but it wasn't an interview. It was more like a date. He asked me to lunch tomorrow."

"So let me see if I get this straight," Cammie said, laying out her concert outfit on the bed. "Probably the hottest guy in the history of rock and roll is more interested in *you* than in being in your little magazine. And the problem is what?"

"The problem is even if something happened . . . even if I liked him . . . he still tours most of the time. I don't even know if he realizes I'm in *high school.* Anyway, it's more than that. I grew up on tours. Trust me, Cam, behind me there's a long line of really beautiful girls who'll do it with him, no strings attached. And I just don't want to join that line. I'm going to cancel lunch."

"You're insane, but I've grown used to it. Oh, your dad came by twice. Said he wants to talk to you."

I rolled my eyes. "My fight with my mother. I'm sure he wants to fix things." I looked at my watch. "No time to settle things now. The bus will be leaving soon."

"Bus?"

"Oh . . . don't get visions of a yellow school bus that smells like old bologna and the cafeteria ladies. Wait until you see."

The two of us got dressed to go over to the arena. At five thirty, we headed down to the lobby and out the doors. There, idling, was a huge tour bus. We climbed on board. Charlie was already there; so were Steve and Greg and George the Vampire. About ten minutes later, my parents and Toby boarded.

"This bus is amazing," Cam said, walking all the way to the back and then up front again. The bus had couches and four televisions with DVDs playing, a bar, a table, and even two beds that could be converted from seats. The Babydolls were all dressed in variations of black jeans and T-shirts. Greg was drinking Jack Daniel's straight from the bottle. He barely acknowledged the rest of the band. Toby gave him a dirty look and sat down next to my father on a

couch—which was a deep cranberry velvet and very soft.
Cam and I went to the bar and poured ourselves diet Cokes.
Music blasted from speakers everywhere, playing—what
else?—the Babydolls' box set compilation—all their top
songs.

"Where are the Wolves?" Cammie asked me quietly.

"They have their own bus."

The bus driver, a roadie everyone called Duke, pulled
out into Tokyo's rush-hour traffic. Cammie and I sat together, and I avoided looking at my parents. My father is always a little tense before a show, so my mother was
rubbing the back of his neck and whispering to him.

The bus windows were tinted black, but we could see
out as little children pointed at the bus and people stared,
I presume wondering who we were. Cammie was excited,
babbling on about each purchase she had made that afternoon.

"You're going to have to ship most of it, Cam. It won't
fit in your suitcase."

"I've already thought of that. I'm going to ship home
my *old* clothes and pack my new ones."

"Like your old clothes were so terrible."

She looked over at Steve Zane and then back at me. "A
girl can't look too hot, Livy."

"Whatever you say. I'm going to take some pictures." I
opened my backpack and pulled out my digital camera. It
was a good camera—Toby had gotten it for me for Christmas. At holidays and birthdays, my father has this unusual
way of being ridiculously extravagant. But he buys me
things I don't necessarily *want*. Like last Christmas he

63

bought me a fur jacket. I don't believe in wearing fur. Or there was my birthday two years ago, when he bought me an exotic snake that cost thousands of dollars. In the first place, I didn't want a snake, no matter how "cool" he thought it was. I had once remarked that a roadie had an amazing snake tattoo—it didn't mean I wanted a slithering pet. In the second place, snakes have to be fed *live* mice and rats. Then you stare at the snake, which has this fat lump in its middle for days. Dad brought it back to the exotic pet store and traded it for a hamster I named Sid Vicious—in the care of our housekeeper, Mrs. Anderson, while we were on the road. Toby, though, always seemed to know what I wanted. He knew one day as a journalist, I'd need a good camera.

"Smile, Cam." I pointed it at her. She immediately struck her best pose, sucking in her cheeks so she looked even *more* like a supermodel. I am the least photogenic person on the planet—I'm a blinker. If I'm lucky enough not to blink, then my picture looks like a mug shot. I'm not ugly, just can't take a picture to save my life. Cammie photographs so each one looks like it belongs in a model's portfolio or in a magazine.

I snapped her picture, and then I took photos of the band. Greg drinking. Steve dozing—my guess because he'd already drunk half a bottle of liquor. My father and Charlie and Toby huddled together, praying. That was a new thing for them. They joined hands to say the Serenity Prayer from AA: *God, grant me the serenity to accept the things I cannot change, the courage to change the things I can, and the wisdom to know the difference.* I knew I couldn't change my family.

We arrived at Tokyo stadium in Chofu, and security waved our bus in. We got off, and the Babydolls all went to their dressing rooms. Cammie, Toby, and I went to check out the stage and the fans who were already arriving.

"Look at them all," Cammie marveled. I snapped some pictures of the stadium as it started filling up. Roadies and stage crew members were doing sound checks.

"You can feel the energy. Come on; let's go grab something to eat, and then we'll stake out a good spot so we can see everything." As much as I hate life on the road, there is something totally electric about waiting for the band to go on. The crowd is like a living, breathing organism, and nowhere are the Babydolls more popular than Japan.

Toby led the way, moving backstage and then down toward the dressing rooms and lounge areas. As we rounded a corner, we spotted two girls flashing their breasts at security, trying to talk their way into the Wolves' dressing room.

"Gross!" Cammie watched as one of the security guys reached out and felt one of the girls' breasts and laughed.

"That's nothing," Toby said. "There are girls who will do anything. Two guys at once, you name it."

"Don't they have any self-respect?"

I shook my head. "Honestly? No. *Now* do you see why I would never want to get involved with a musician?"

Cammie looked at me. "Not all of them are like that, Livy."

"As a matter of fact, they are."

"Livy," Cam said, "you would *hate* it if someone tried to stereotype you that way."

We walked by the girls. I tried not to stare. We rounded another corner, and there were Nick and Kai and the other two members of the Wolves—surrounded by about ten girls.

"Livy," Nick called out to me, but I pretended I didn't hear him. I wasn't sure why, except that it made me feel awful to see him with all those girls around.

We got to the Babydolls' lounge. A big buffet table had been set up. As I took a plate and began to pick up some appetizers—sushi, chicken satay, crisp celery and ranch dressing—Cammie elbowed me.

"Why didn't you say hi to him? That was rude."

"He was busy."

"You are so stubborn, Livy James. I know you like him."

"I don't."

I took my plate and went to sit down. George came into the room.

"All right, guys . . ." He held his hands up. "This is the tour that the world's been waiting for. I want to see you blow the fucking stadium away."

That seemed to be the cue for Greg to take another huge swig of whiskey. My father snapped, "Do you have to do the show loaded, Greg?"

Greg's dark brown eyes flashed anger. "It was never a problem before."

"Well, maybe it is now."

"I just love your holier-than-thou crap. Sure, I'll stop drinking," Greg yelled, and threw the bottle against the wall, where it shattered. My mother jumped, and Cam let out a little scream. Greg sneered, "Just because you hopped on the rehab bandwagon doesn't mean you can preach to me, Paul. I knew you when you were a thousand times more fucked up than me."

My father stood. Greg stood. They faced off against each other, with George in the middle holding them apart. Toby and Charlie grabbed my father, and Toby said, "Come on, guys. Don't start the tour this way."

Greg started laughing—nothing was funny, but that didn't seem to make a difference. He walked over to some girl he'd picked up and kissed her on the mouth. "Come on, Danielle; let's go watch the opening act."

They left, and an uneasy silence filled the room. I whispered to Cam, "Let's go; I want to take some pictures of the Wolves."

"I thought you didn't like him."

"I don't. But I still need to e-mail pictures to *Rock On*."

We left and traveled down the hall, passing the two girls we saw before, now buttoned up and wearing backstage passes.

"So letting someone touch your breasts gets you backstage?" Cammie asked after we passed them.

"No, but I'm sure a blow job does."

"Have I ever told you it's a miracle you're semi-normal?"

"Yup. And you're right."

We showed our passes backstage, and as we got closer, the roar of the crowd was deafening.

"I thought the Japanese were so conservative," Cammie said.

"They like their rock and roll as much as the Americans, and this is the first time the Babydolls have *ever* appeared here. And the Wolves are really hot right now because of the new album."

I grabbed Cammie's hand and pulled her into the wings of the stage. An announcer was speaking in Japanese. I recognized "the Wolves"—and from a rising platform, the four members of the band appeared with their instruments, fog-machine smoke billowing around their ankles. Nick ran to the front of the stage, and the crowd was so loud I couldn't even hear myself speak. I tapped Cammie and smiled—our own sign language. I could see how excited she was.

Nick began singing, opening with the song "Tuesday at Ten" that he told me was his favorite.

> *Tuesday at ten*
> *Spinning backward again*
> *I know I should leave*
> *But you're becoming a friend*

Cammie started dancing in place. I snapped pictures with my digital camera. I zoomed the lens and could see Nick so close up that his tattoo was clear when he turned his head.

And suddenly I got it. His voice was a growl, and he moved on the stage like he was making love with the microphone. Only that's not really it. He was projecting so much more than making love. More like sex—hot, crazy sex. The kind I'd only read about. He was glistening already with sweat, and his intensity was electrifying. I got goose bumps on my arms, and the back of my neck felt prickly and hot.

My whole life, the Babydolls had been a part of my world. But because I knew them all, because I knew them in so much detail, they were just this crazy dysfunctional family to me. But there on the stage, I felt something for a singer that I never had before. I'd always loved music—in my head, in my words. But now a singer had made himself part of me. He was in me—mixed in with the words and his voice.

The Wolves played seven songs, and I couldn't take my eyes off of them. Nick was the star, of course, but Kai was amazing, too. They all were.

Then Nick took a bow and stood still at the microphone. "I know most of you won't understand me . . . speaking in English."

Over the stadium sound system, we could hear his voice coming back at us, echoing over the valley of people.

"This last song is called 'Head in the Clouds,' and I'd like to dedicate it to a very beautiful girl who saw the magic of Mount Fuji today."

He began singing. I turned a bright shade of red. Cammie pinched my arm.

"Ouch!"

"If you don't break your no-musicians rule, I'll never speak to you again," she screamed into my ear.

"Is that a promise?"

"Very funny." She was shouting, and her voice sounded hoarse and strained.

After the Wolves got off the stage, there was a brief break as the set was changed. Then the Babydolls started with "Long, Dark Tunnel." The crowd went even wilder. I could tell my father and Greg weren't speaking to each other. My father kept turning his back to Greg as he sang. But the crowd didn't notice the lack of harmony in the band. They were screaming too much. Baby-doll pajamas and thongs were thrown onstage. Two women threw bouquets of roses. It looked like a few women—and one guy—fainted in the front couple of rows.

A few songs into the Babydolls concert, Nick and Kai came up to Cammie and me.

"You guys were great!" Cammie shouted. We resorted to sign language—since Kai and Nick both had earplugs in. I made a note to get Cammie and me earplugs. Everyone in rock and roll has heard stories of Pete Townsend of the Who losing nearly all his hearing from years of deafeningly loud concerts.

I snapped pictures and tried not to think about Nick Hoffman and how he made me feel when he was onstage. When the final song came, and then two encores, the stadium lit up, and exhausted fans began inching their way to the exits.

"You girls up for a night out in Tokyo?" Kai asked Cammie and me. My ears were still ringing, and we all started making our way to the backstage area and then the dressing room. Before we could even answer, we were swarmed. Girls—ready to party and handpicked by, my guess, George the Vampire—came over to Kai and Nick asking for autographs, some doing the "sign my naked breast with a Sharpie" routine.

"Come on, Cam," I whispered. "Let's just go."

In the distance, I could see my father and Charlie and Toby.

"Come on, Cam, Liv. Let's get on the bus," Toby said. He put his hand tightly on my elbow and steered me to the exit. My father and Charlie were close behind. My mom, I could see, was already up ahead of us. I felt rushed, and Cammie was teetering in her heels to keep up.

"What's going on?" I asked.

"Don't look back," Toby muttered.

But of course, I had to.

Steve Zane and Greg Essex were pouring shots between the breasts of two girls and licking the whiskey off of them.

"Nothing like a good breast shot," Dad muttered. "Assholes."

Toby looked over at me and Cammie. "If I *ever* catch either of you girls behaving like that, I swear I'll pack you into boxes and ship you straight home."

"Come on, Toby, that looks like so much fun," I teased. "*Please* let me be a slut. Pretty please."

"Yeah," Cammie piped up. "It's something I could write home to my parents about. They'd be so proud."

Toby cracked a smile, and we reached the bus. Mom was already lying on a sofa with a chenille blanket tossed over her lap. I saw her open her purse and pop two aspirin with a diet Coke.

Cammie and I settled into a pair of captain's chairs. "How are Greg and Steve getting back to the hotel?" she asked.

Toby stood near us as the bus driver pulled away from

the stadium. "We always have a limo on standby for this kind of thing. Just in case."

"Oh," she said, and leaned back in her chair. She made it recline and plugged in a pair of earphones. "I'm going to watch TV," she said. We had a DVD of *Reservoir Dogs* on. It's my father's favorite movie.

While she watched the screen, my father paced—seeing people drinking and out of control was hard for him. Me? It made me positive I never wanted to make a fool of myself like that. Him? Made him want to join in. Charlie was chain-smoking. My mother had her eyes shut. Toby went to talk to my dad. He poured him a club soda, sat next to him, and patted him on the back.

I put my digital camera on my lap and started reviewing pictures. I'd have to pick the best ones to send to Carl. I clicked through and spotted one. Nick's eyes were shut, and he was clearly screaming out some lyric . . . and it was as if I were back there watching him again. I felt goose bumps. I didn't want to send the picture to Carl. I'd send another one. This one felt too personal.

I decided to download it to my laptop and keep it for a while. I wasn't sure why, but I wanted the picture to belong to only me.

Chapter Nine

"2:45 A.M."
—Elliott Smith

TO: Carl Erikson
CC: Rob Hernandez
FR: Livy James
RE: Postcard from Tokyo/JPEG
attachment

Hi, Carl.

It's almost three o'clock in the morning, and I can't sleep. It's the time difference. And it's the concert. It was amazing. Attached is a picture of the Wolves and one of the Babydolls taken at Tokyo Stadium. Here's what I wrote to go along with it. . . .

> *Everyone who loves music has that moment. That instant in time when you were a kid and you heard a rock song that got you. Really got you down in your soul. You saved your money for the CD—this was before file sharing. Then, bringing home your precious CD, you unwrapped that pesky cellophane (I always had to use*

73

my teeth) and popped the CD into your Discman or put it on your boom box.

Something happened.

Music, before that moment, was music. It was there to sing along with, hum along to, dance to, move to. It was a sound track for your life. But this was different. This one song, whatever it was, transformed you. The song took you someplace primal, someplace where you would never be the same.

Last night in Tokyo Stadium, the Wolves and the Babydolls kicked off their international tour. I've grown up around rock all my life. I heard it in the womb even, as my father, Paul James, sang to my mother's stomach. But last night, I and tens of thousands of Japanese fans heard something so primal that we're forever changed by the experience. It was the kind of show where, for those who were there, it's imprinted on the brain forever. Sort of like what our parents say about Woodstock—the first one.

Nick Hoffman became the music. Paul James has always been the music. That's what people say. You have to see the Babydolls live to know their music. Now the same holds true for the Wolves. You just have to see them. You have to see him to get it. James and Hoffman both have the spark.

If you go back throughout the history of rock and roll, there have been a few lead singers you cannot take your eyes off of and you cannot stop listening to. Elvis Presley—the thin, hip-swiveling one, not the sequined-jumpsuit one—supposedly had it. Mick Jagger. You can hate INXS—but if you ever saw the late Michael Hutchence onstage, he was magnetic. I think Eddie Vedder has it. Gwen Stefani is a female rocker who's got that something. Chrissie Hynde will still tell the world to fuck off from the stage—but you will still watch her.

In an MTV lip-synched world, they all have the divine gift that Britney Spears and Ashlee Simpson would kill to have. And last night Paul James and Nick Hoffman proved once and for all that they are rock stars, not packaged product. They are the music they sing.

Chapter Ten

The next morning, Cammie and I ordered croissants and coffee from room service. We ate at a table by our window, overlooking the city. Mount Fuji kept her guard in the distance.

"You were up late," Cam said, taking a bite of a croissant smeared with raspberry jam.

"I couldn't sleep. So I wrote to Carl and sent him some pictures I took."

"You couldn't sleep because you *want* him."

"Who?"

Cammie took a sip of coffee. "You know, Livy, we've been best friends since I lobbed an eraser at you in social studies five years ago. You can't fool me."

"All right, all right. I like him. I like him a lot, Cam, but I'm not going to do something stupid."

"Have you ever stopped to think that maybe he's not like your father? Or Fred Durst. Or whoever you think just lines up the women. Maybe he's really just a nice guy. And . . . you know, you really need to relax. Don't worry if he is or isn't this jerky rock star. Go ahead and have a summer fling. You might have *fun*."

"Well, whether I like it or not, I have to go to lunch with him today. Last night while I was writing Carl, I listened to the tape of my interview. There's just not enough to use. I have nothing to write about. What did I find out, for God's sake? I know he's a Buddhist, but that's about it. Oh, and he can drive a Vespa. And I know what his tattoo means. But I can't write a whole story about that."

"Sounds like enough to me."

I threw a sugar cube at her. "Try to pretend like you get what journalism is all about. Anyway, today I'm going to get him to focus and answer some more questions so I can do an article on him and get it over with. I still need to interview Greg Essex, Steve Zane—and both my parents at some point. I need to finish writing about the Babydolls."

"Hey, did you hear the phone ring?"

"No."

"Well, the light on our phone is blinking. Maybe when you were in the shower and I was still sleeping. But I swear I didn't hear it."

I shrugged and stood and went to the phone. An electronic voice let me press seven to get the commands in English: then I was able to retrieve the message.

"Your message from one-oh-five A.M.: 'Hi, Livy. This is Nick. We got separated backstage. I really wanted to talk to you. I'll see you for lunch tomorrow . . . uh, today, I guess. It's one in the morning. I hope you liked the concert. Good night.' "

"Who was it?" Cam asked.

"Nick. Just confirming lunch. Must have come in before we got home last night."

We finished breakfast and called Toby. Cammie and Toby made plans to sightsee. When he got to our room, I told him not to let Cammie buy so much as a postcard.

"You're entirely too responsible, Liv." Cammie pouted.

"I mean it. Not one thing. Look at this place!" I showed Toby all the packages.

"I know. I tried to tell her yesterday, but it was like she was possessed. I mean, I've faced down a thousand shrieking girls pounding on the windows of a limousine, but that *pales* in comparison to Cammie in a store."

Cammie stuck her tongue out at him. Dressed in jeans and a T-shirt from the Gap, she grabbed her backpack and camera and they left. I had twenty minutes until lunch and went in to finish putting on my makeup. Every time I thought about Nick Hoffman onstage, I got the same feeling, a cross between goose bumps and a shiver. And maybe a tiny bit like I was going to puke. I took a deep breath and grabbed my backpack and took the elevator to the lobby.

He was waiting. He had on jeans and a T-shirt with the symbol for yin and yang on it. He waved when he saw me, and when I walked over to him he kissed me on the cheek.

"Good to see you, Liv." His slight Irish accent made everything he said sort of sound musical.

"Thanks."

"Come on, off for another surprise."

I half expected the Vespa to be sitting there, but it was a black stretch limousine—a Mercedes-Benz, no less. The driver stood by the rear passenger door, opened it, and I climbed inside. A small bouquet of miniature roses sat waiting for me on the seat. This was more like a date. And that made me feel like I was going to be sick for sure.

I went out with Chris Carlson for eight months, and never once did he make me feel like I was going to puke.

Chris and I had made out—a lot—he was an amazing kisser, and we even talked about doing it. We didn't, mostly because I really liked him, but I was sure I didn't love him. Unlike Cammie, I was going to lose my virginity to someone I really loved. But the thought of kissing Nick, or even touching him, made me want to heave. I mean, what kind of writer throws up on her interview subject? I bet no one at *Rolling Stone* ever did that.

Nick climbed in back, and the driver got in the front seat and pulled away from the hotel.

"Thanks for the flowers."

"You're welcome. I felt really bad last night."

"Why? The concert was great."

"But you and Cammie took off so soon. One minute you were there, and the next you were gone."

I looked out the window.

"What is it, Livy? Didn't you have a good time yesterday?"

"Sure. But you know, that whole backstage scene just isn't me."

"It's not me, either. Or Kai. I swear it. Look at me."

Look at him. Easy for him to say. I took a deep breath and looked his way. Why did he have to have these beautiful eyes? And his eyelashes were longer than mine.

"Get to know me, Liv. Give me a chance. Okay?"

"Okay."

"Good." He grabbed my hand.

"Where are we going?"

"I told you. My favorite restaurant."

About five minutes later the driver pulled up in front

of a deep-red door with no number on it, no sign, nothing to distinguish it from the other doors and buildings on the street.

"Is this it?" I asked.

"Prepare to leave the rest of the world on the sidewalk."

We climbed out of the limousine, and Nick held my hand as we walked to the door. He opened it, and I stepped inside.

I blinked my eyes to help them adjust to the dim interior. It felt ten degrees cooler inside, and it was as tranquil and peaceful as the temple we had visited the day before. A hostess came to us and bowed.

"Reservation for Hoffman," Nick said, bowing as well.

She nodded and motioned for us to follow her. She slid aside a rice-paper wall, and we stepped into a courtyard garden with koi ponds, waterfalls, and bamboo growing. On the other side of the garden we passed into a stone-floored corridor that led to our own little room. She pushed aside another rice-paper wall, and nodded for us to leave our shoes outside. I took off my sneakers, and Nick took off his boots, and we stepped into the room and sat down on crimson silk cushions on either side of a low table. The hostess bowed again, slid the door shut, and we were alone.

"This place is beautiful," I whispered.

"Peaceful."

I nodded. "Are we the only ones here?"

"No, but there aren't many rooms. It's very expensive— you have to be someone who wants to pay for this kind of privacy and tranquillity. To me, it's worth it."

"You'd never know there's a busy city just outside."

"Exactly. Liv?"

"Hmm?"

"You know, like, that scene last night . . . that is not me at all. I spend a lot of energy, a lot of time, trying to carve out a space that's just for me."

I nodded. "I know. My room at home, it's the whole top floor of our house, and it overlooks the water. It's always been a place I could hide from the rest of the world and just write."

"Why do you write about music? Why not about other things?"

"Music has just always been around me. Early on my father tried to brainwash me with the Rolling Stones and the Who, the Kinks. The Clash. He taught me the history of rock. Then he took me back into the blues. Jazz. Muddy Waters. John Lee Hooker. Coltrane. Of course, disco was from the dark side. The Bee Gees had signed a pact with Satan, that sort of thing."

"Well, of course everyone knows that." We both laughed.

"After a while I started really getting into it. I formed my own opinions. I loved finding some band no one had ever heard of and getting all my friends to like them, getting my father to like them. I told him about the Wolves before he ever heard you guys. He hates rap, but you know, I got him to listen to the Beastie Boys and Eminem. NWA. I tried to open up his mind a little. The Strokes. The White Stripes. It was a way to talk to my father."

The door to our room slid open and a waitress brought

in piping-hot towels. We ordered sake and sushi. The wait-ress lit a single candle on our table and then left.

"Is your father hard to talk to?"

"Not really. It's just that he's always a little bit in his own world. I decided a long time ago that his musical ge-nius just takes up so much space in his head that there's no room for the practical stuff of real life, like remembering to come to my school play, or figuring out how to make him-self a cup of coffee. He doesn't even know how to use the coffeemaker. My mother has tried to show him a few times, but it's as though he pulls this stuff on purpose so she'll take care of him. Me, too. And Toby. He's like our big rock-star baby."

"Does that make you mad?"

I shook my head. "It used to. My mother was so busy taking care of him that there wasn't anyone taking care of me. But after a while, I liked the independence, I guess. They let me have a lot of space, and I suppose I'm just lucky that I never got into a lot of trouble."

"I was damn independent too. I left home at fifteen. Been on my own since me and Kai."

"Really? What are your parents like?" I asked. "Do they like your music?"

"Hell, no. They think it's rot."

"But you guys are amazing. I mean, even if they don't like the music, the lyrics are well crafted."

"My da—that's what we call 'father' in Ireland—he just didn't see it that way. Before we fine-tuned our sound, I went through a whole shaved-head, piercing stage. He thought I was bollocks. Besides this tattoo"—he ran his hand along his neck—"I've got one on my stomach. One on my leg. He didn't understand that sometimes you're just expressing yourself the best way you know how when you're that age."

"They must be proud of you now. You're rich. Famous. On the radio."

He shook his head. "I'm afraid not, Livy. But how about you? Are your parents proud of you bein' in the magazine?"

I nodded and felt a little guilty that I had fought with my mother. "They *are* proud. My mom is quieter about it. I don't know. Cammie thinks she's jealous that I'm getting to follow my dream. She was a singer once. I haven't heard her sing in years."

"Didn't she used to sing backup for the Babydolls?"

I nodded. "But you know all the rumors. After Paris, I don't think she ever sang again."

Our sake arrived, and we clinked cups together.

"To Mount Fuji."

I smiled. "To Mount Fuji."

The rest of the lunch flew by. We talked about music and traveling. He was very involved in the Free Tibet movement and dreamed of one day going there. He taught me more about Buddhism. I forgot my interview questions and just got lost in the conversation. Some journalist. Eventually it was three thirty and the check arrived. He handed his AmEx card to the waitress. When she shut the door, he stood and came over to my side of the table and sat down on the cushion next to me.

"You going to the concert tonight?"

I nodded. This was it. He was going to kiss me. I prayed to his Buddha. I prayed to God. *Please, please, dear God, don't make me faint. Or throw up.*

"Remember that I'll sing 'Head in the Clouds' for you."

I nodded. And then I shut my eyes as he leaned in and kissed me. He pulled me really close and kissed me harder. As kisses go, it even beat kissing Cammie's older brother, with whom I once shared an incredible make-out session before we both decided it was crazy.

The rice-paper door slid aside, and we stopped kissing long enough for him to sign the receipt. Then we kissed some more. My heart felt like it was pounding so loud that he could hear it. I put my hand to his chest—and I could feel his heart pounding, too. Eventually we stopped and just looked into each other's eyes. Finally he stood and helped me up, and we left through the beautiful gardens. Just before we exited the restaurant, I turned around.

"What, Livy? You forget something?"

"No. I just wish that sometimes the world would stand still. I wish we could stay here."

"Me, too," he whispered, and took my hand, kissing my neck and leading me back out into the busy Tokyo streets.

Chapter Eleven

"Starf_ _ _ _ _ _, Inc."
                —Nine Inch Nails

Toby was very clever. On our last night in Tokyo, after the concert, he invited Kai and Nick to come along as Cam and I and Toby trekked all over the city. Toby was determined that Cam would have nothing to do with Steve Zane. The night before, after we had seen Steve and Greg do shots off of those girls, Toby told me that the two of them and one of the stage crew had taken eight girls by limousine back to the hotel, where they partied until six o'clock in the morning. When they tried to order more liquor from room service, the manager of the hotel came up and found the room trashed, with naked girls passed out on the floor. The only thing that kept him from throwing us *all* out was that we had only one more night scheduled. And George the Vampire is a smooth talker. He promised to babysit them.

Cammie seemed oblivious to Toby's plan, and she looked really happy as we drove to video arcades, karaoke bars, and shopping areas. Kai looked thrilled to be with Cam, and Nick and I in general made everyone sick, kissing and holding hands. I no longer felt like I was going to throw up if he kissed me—but being apart from him kind of made me sick to my stomach now. We just fit together.

I knew I was breaking every rule about musicians, but

I also knew *he* broke all the rules about musicians. He wasn't a stoner, he didn't do drugs, and he wasn't interested in the groupie scene. My God, he was a musician who thought about *karma*. When I was with him, I was happy, and I suppose that was more important than my rule.

But all good things must come to an end, and the next day we were leaving Tokyo for London. While we were there, Cam and I planned to go to my grandparents' house in Canterbury for a night. I saw my mother's parents only every year or so, and my mother had no plans to see them at all—things had always been strained between them. Or at least for as long as I could remember.

Nick was excited because London and its clubs and pubs were his "stomping grounds," as he called them. We made plans to meet up at the hotel in London, and said good-bye, making out for fifteen minutes in the hall until George the Vampire came and found him. They had a different plane schedule than the Babydolls did. All of the Babydolls' schedules were set for afternoons. George the Vampire had learned, after twenty-two years, that there was no way to get any of the Babydolls up before noon.

Around one o'clock, I told Cam I was going to go try to get an interview with Greg Essex.

"I'm just going to see if I can catch him. I know he won't want to do it, but even if he gives me twenty minutes, I can write the next part of the Babydolls' story on the plane and send it when I get to London."

She was sitting on her suitcase, trying to get it to close. "Are you going to ask him about that night in Paris? You know, when he tried to shoot your father?"

"No. I don't think so. I mean, what's he supposed to say? 'I shot at your father. Oops. Sorry.' I actually want to hear more about when they first started. . . . And, um . . . I think you'd better call Toby to try to close that."

I opened my journal to see the notes I had on Greg.

> Greg Essex
> Member of the Babydolls
> Instrument: Guitar, can also play the piano (uses it to compose only)
> Miscellaneous: Major drug user, including a past history of heroin use; womanizer; heavy binge drinker—Jack Daniel's is drink of choice; key reason for the band breaking up; used to date Mom; shot at Dad in the infamous "Night in Paris" episode; has never spoken on the record about why he shot at him.

I grabbed my tape recorder and walked down the hall to Greg's suite. He was on the opposite end of the hotel floor from my parents. Smart thinking.

I knocked on the door.

"Who the fuck is it?"

"Um . . . Greg? It's Livy."

"Damn . . . shit . . . piss . . . Hold on."

I heard him fumbling with the lock, and Greg appeared in a plush hotel robe and boxer shorts, looking horrible. His hair was sticking up wildly, his complexion was greenish yellow, and he had circles under his eyes. His room smelled like stale vomit and cigarettes. I wasn't sure if *Rock On* wanted me to write about the *real* lives of rock and rollers. I didn't think people wanted to read about the hangovers. The mornings after.

"Um . . . I thought maybe you'd be ready to leave. I'm sorry to bother you."

"No, come on in, Liv. Coffee?"

I shook my head.

"What's up, Liv? Your father send you in here to make peace?"

I hesitated. "No-o. I . . . well, I don't know if you heard, but I'm planning on going to NYU for journalism. And I got a job this summer writing for *Rock On,* about the tour. I was wondering if I could interview you for twenty minutes, tops. I brought my tape recorder. Please say yes. *Please.*"

He looked at me. "Hmm. Sure. Hold on, though." He motioned me over to the couch, shut the door behind me, and then disappeared into the bathroom. When he emerged, he looked much better, his face washed, his hair combed.

He came and sat down next to me on the couch. "Shoot."

I turned on the tape recorder.

"What attracted you to the other three members of the band at first?"

"Well, I just wanted to make music. I wanted to get laid, frankly."

"That's it? You formed one of the world's greatest rock bands so you could meet women? You wanted girls?"

"Sex, drugs, and rock and roll! Long live rock. All the rest of that crap. I wanted to kick ass onstage, play my guitar, and have orgies. I mean, I wanted the whole life that goes along with having a hit record."

That wasn't the inspirational music story I wanted to write, but I'd have to go with it.

"When did you realize you'd really made it, that you were a phenomenon?"

"That's easy. When I could behave any way I wanted and get away with it. I could smash my television set in my hotel room, roll a joint in a restaurant, look at a girl and she'd come running. I could do whatever I wanted and I was Greg Rock Star Essex. No one could say anything to me. And if they did, I didn't give a shit anyway."

"So the music didn't mean anything to you? None of the songs?"

He shrugged.

"Okay. So why do you think you guys broke up?"

The question hung in the air. He looked at me until I was about to say, *Forget it,* and then he started talking.

"You really don't know?"

"No. I mean, I know you fired a gun at my father. I know you used to go out with my mother. But you were a huge star, and then you just walked away from it all."

He took a pack of cigarettes from the coffee table and lit one. He started smoking and blowing smoke rings, and I felt really uncomfortable.

"I'm sorry. I actually didn't intend to ask about that night."

"I didn't date your mother, Livy. I *loved* her. Big difference. Do you even know the difference at your age?" He sounded accusing.

"Yes!"

"Not this kind of love. I loved her until I . . . Aw, Christ . . . look at my wrists."

He rolled up the sleeves of his bathrobe, and I could see faint scars on the inside of both wrists.

"I loved her until the only way I could show her how much was to try to kill myself right in her presence."

"What?" I felt like the room had just gotten twenty degrees colder. No one had ever told me this. No one.

"That's right." He raised his voice a little bit. "I loved her, Livy. Your father didn't."

My voice trembling, I whispered, "Yes, he did. He did love her. I know he loved her. He helped her get over you when you cheated on her." I felt panicky.

"Bullshit. Fucking bullshit. That's what they want everyone to believe, Livy." I could see in his eyes that he delighted in shocking me, maybe in hurting me. He said it in a taunting way. "*I* know the truth. Your mother and father know the truth, but they think it sounds better the way they tell it. Let Greg be the prick. Let Greg be the bad guy."

His hands shook as he took a deep drag off his cigarette. "You won't have the guts to print this." He leaned in closer to the tape recorder and shouted, "Listen up! I loved your mother. I loved Anna. And more than that—I could see she was talented. She was so incredibly talented, Livy."

"My mother? Singing, right?"

"No, not just singing." I think he saw he was scaring me and he settled down a little. "Songwriting. And her voice. She had more talent in her little finger than the entire band had in . . . all of us. Her voice was like Janis Joplin's. Raw. Real. And unlike Janis, she projected sexuality onstage in a way that . . . No one could hold a candle to her, Liv. No one. She would have been huge. Huge."

90

My mother? I mean, was this the mother who thought gardening was the meaning of life? Who drove our housekeeper crazy with a long, anal-retentive list of precisely how to iron my father's shirts and prepare his lunch just so? The woman who thought I played my music too loud so she had my room soundproofed?

"Add to that tremendous voice her beauty. Add to that she could outwrite us all. Her lyrics were works of art. She was brilliant."

He paused and passed his hand across his face. "Forget I brought it up." He angrily stubbed out his cigarette and then lit another.

"No . . . what happened?" I couldn't help but ask.

"I knew one day you would come to me. I knew you'd ask. Your mom and I wrote some songs together and your father didn't want to sing them. None of them. If he didn't have a hand in the song, he vetoed it, and George was too afraid of pissing off his lead singer."

"You wrote songs with my mother?"

"Yes. Better songs than the Babydolls have ever sung. She actually wrote most of them—more of them. I smoothed them a bit."

"That doesn't sound like my father."

"Doesn't it? He *has* to be the center of attention. She takes care of him like he's a child." He seemed to be mad again, sneering.

I didn't say anything because I felt sick. It *did* sound like him.

"Liv . . . I cheated on her. Yes. I broke her heart. But it didn't mean anything. I begged her for a second chance. I

91

slit my wrists while she watched me. The pain was so intense *inside* that I had to show her by doing something on the outside."

"Oh my God . . ."

"Yeah. Oh my God. So she wrapped my wrists in towels and got me to a doctor. She said she'd think it over. She loved me. She loved me crazy, Liv. And the thing is, I wanted to help her. I wanted the whole world to see what I saw, this amazing talent. This amazing woman. My lover. My love." He was as mercurial as people always said, one minute poignant, the next nasty, then back again.

A combination of shock and anger overwhelmed me. I wasn't sure how my parents—my mother in particular—could keep all these details hidden. Didn't I deserve to know the truth? I was the baby that resulted from all this craziness. For a minute or two I was silent, just trying to absorb what he said.

"She never told me. I knew she could sing, but . . ."

"That's where you get your writing talent from, Liv. Not your father. Your mother is the gifted one. But she hides her gifts, and it's disgusting. A waste. Christ, you think I don't know it's luck, bullshit luck that makes us as huge as we are? Luck, some talent, good looks, your father's stage presence. I know. I get stoned, wasted, drunk, and it's no waste of talent. I'm nothing. Not like her, Liv."

"So . . . you and she never got back together?"

"No. Your father, he wanted her. He wanted her because *I* had her. That's the kind of relationship we had, like two brothers who love each other but hate each other. He wanted to take her away from me. He wanted her because . . . I don't know. She was different. She wasn't like the other girls hanging around. She had it. Whatever that magic is. And he didn't want to record anyone else's songs. So while I was recovering and trying to sober up and get my act together and begging her to come back to me, he won her heart. So I just did what came naturally. I tried to hurt her. Cheated again, asked her to do a toss in the hay with me and another girl. I wanted to hurt her. And him."

"Is that why you shot at my father?"

He laughed and sneered at me. "Haven't you been *listening?* What kind of journalist are you? No. They think that's why I went after him, but hell, no. I thought you were mine, Liv. But she married him, and I had to wait five or six months like the rest of the world to see who you belonged to. You were his. And that hurt like hell. But what hurt the most was this festering illness inside me—this feeling of dread that your father would never let her shine. He would keep her next to him like some prize. The rock star with the beautiful wife. And he'd buy her things and they'd live the life. But he'd never let her gift out there—because he *knew* she was better than he was. Better than all of us, Livy. And he couldn't take two stars in the family. And that made me insane."

"So you thought *shooting* him was a solution?"

"I just told you I was nuts. I was doing heroin. I was drunk all the time. I got loaded one night and tried to kill him. I wanted to free her."

He stubbed out his cigarette and leaned over, grabbing at his head. "Fuck!"

I didn't know what to say. It was as if the entire story of my life and my parents' lives had just been pulled apart.

"Greg?"

"What?"

"Greg, I'm sorry."

"What are you sorry for?"

"All this time, I guess I saw you as the bad guy. The way you are with the groupies and the drugs and the way you act sometimes. I just didn't know."

"Yeah, well sometimes there's more to these little fairy tales, the bad guys versus the good guys. Everyone just thinks it's easier to go on pretending it's about something it's not."

I reached out to take his hand, and I shut off my tape recorder. I had just scored the rock-and-roll scoop of the year, and I wasn't sure I wanted it. Greg took his other hand and tousled my hair.

"I would have loved for you to have been mine, Liv. I can see your talent. I've read the stuff you show Toby."

There was a knock on the door that startled both of us.

"Bet it's George the Vampire," I said.

He laughed. "That what you call him now? Good name."

He stood and walked over to the door and opened it. There stood my mother. And without a word, she hauled off and backhanded him across the face with all her might.

Chapter Twelve

"You fucker!" she screamed, and stormed into the room. "You couldn't have me, so now you're trying to fuck my daughter? Low, even for you, Greg."

Greg shut the door and slipped off his robe so he was standing in just boxer shorts. "Nice to see you, too, Anna. I see that backhand of yours is as powerful as ever." The broken man, the man who'd just told me his story, was gone. The sneering Greg Essex who liked to cause trouble was standing there. This was going to get ugly.

"Mom . . . it's not what you think."

"Livy . . . I told you, you don't know everything. So this is what you do? I tell you to stay away from Nick Hoffman, and I find you here with *Greg,* the lowest of the low? I went to your room—Cammie told me you came here to talk to him. What kind of lies did he tell you?"

"No," I said, standing up. "No . . . Mom, it's not like that. This is for the magazine. It's important to me."

"No, you're right, Anna." Greg sauntered over to me and threw his arm around my shoulder, his voice laced with sarcasm. "We were just going to have a toss in the hay. I sampled the fruits of the mother, why not the daughter?"

My mother picked up an ashtray and hurled it against the wall. "Over my dead body, Greg. Where's your gun, big

95

man? You bring it on this trip so you could try to kill *me* this time?"

"No. I figure the real way to hurt you is through Livy."

"I mean it, Greg. I mean it. You touch a hair on her head, and I'll kill you."

I looked at Greg's face, and I felt like I could read his mind. He wondered how my mother could have come to doubt him so much. Weren't his wrists proof enough? But I could see his eyes were past all reason. He and my mother were locked in a battle that began before I was born, destined to keep hurting each other. At that moment, he grabbed me and kissed me hard, his tongue probing my mouth as I pushed desperately to get away.

My mother screamed. I grabbed my tape recorder and my mother's arm.

"Come on, Mom, we're getting out of here."

I almost didn't recognize her. Her eyes were wild, and she seethed at him. "This isn't over, Greg. When I tell Paul, he'll finish this."

"Tell him. Please tell him," Greg said with an evil-looking smile on his face. Then he held his wrists up in the air. "Tell him."

I had no idea if my mother got the meaning. Next Greg dropped his boxer shorts so he was standing there naked as I pulled her to the door, opened it, and tried to drag her outside.

"Tell him!" Greg screamed as I slammed the door between us.

My mother took a few steps away from me and collapsed to the floor, sobbing.

"Mom . . . Mom . . . it's not what you think."

"You've been—" she gasped for air between sobs—"running around with that Nick Hoffman. Liv, this isn't the life for you. Be a writer. Be something, but don't end up just following some band around like I did. It'll ruin your life . . . break your heart."

"Mom . . . you don't even know me."

I pressed rewind and put the tape recorder on the floor. Greg's voice soon started speaking, softly at first. My mother stopped crying. She looked shocked, and her face was so pale I thought she might faint. When the tape was done, I pressed stop.

"I know, Mom. I know the truth now." I picked up the tape recorder and walked away. Nothing—not my mother, father, or the Babydolls themselves—was what it once seemed.

Chapter Thirteen

TO: Carl Erikson
FR: Livy James
RE: Postcard from Tokyo

Hi, Carl.

Things here are really strange, and I don't know who to talk to. I have to ask you something. I got an interview with Greg Essex, and it was nothing like I expected. It was about the breakup, that night in Paris, and so much more. You've known Greg and my father and mother since before I was even born. Why do you think Greg tried to shoot my father that night?

Please write me back. I am really confused.

Hugs,

Livy

Chapter Fourteen

TO: Livy James
FR: Carl Erikson
RE: Postcard from Tokyo

Hi, Livy.

Yes, I've known your parents a long, long time. I was one of only ten people who attended their wedding in their backyard—they were living in L.A. at the time. Your mother looked stunning. Dressed in a cream-colored slip dress, she was glowing—pregnant with you—and reminded me of a fairy in A Midsummer Night's Dream.

Liv, the only people who really know what happened are Greg, your mother, and your father. Over the years I've tried to stay neutral, to stay out of it. I've heard the official story, of course. It's been repeated often enough that everyone assumes it's true. But I've always guessed there was more. I'm not sure why, except I knew Greg before your mother left him, and I knew him after. He has never been the same.

Journalists face a tough task. Sometimes, it seems so much easier to simply keep retelling the same story over and over. But are you more committed to the truth or the fairy tale? And just because you find out the "truth," does that mean it's right to print it? Or that it's even true? Here's one of the hardest lessons a journalist can learn: Maybe each of them thinks he or she knows the truth. Maybe because it's the truth to each of them.

Liv, I know whatever you write will be fantastic, and you'll be true to your heart as a writer. If I can help, call me or e-mail me. I believe in you, Livy. Hang in there.

Rock On,

Carl

Chapter Fifteen

"I Just Don't Know What to Do with Myself"
—The White Stripes

I didn't play the tape for Cammie right away. On the plane
to London I put on my earphones and listened to it over
and over again, shutting my eyes and picturing Greg. I un-
derstood what Carl was saying—that there were three
truths: my father's, my mother's, and Greg's. But the thing
that was so hard was that I believed Greg. And a little piece
of my heart broke for him.

When she didn't know it, when she was sleeping, I
would look at my mom. You could tell she had been crying
a lot. Her face was blotchy, and her eyes were puffy. My father always said she was a beautiful woman but an ugly
crier.

After I played the tape a hundred times, I thought about
maybe telling Nick. I didn't know what to tell him if I did.
Most of all, right now, I felt alone.

Greg sat as far away from me and my mother as possible. No one thought this was strange, because they always
avoided each other. My father and Toby sat together. I wondered if my father really did have to be the star, if he had
really kept my mother from becoming a famous singer and
songwriter in her own right. I wished the plane afforded
more privacy, because I knew that Toby would have some
good advice for me.

Toby Quinn
Bodyguard/driver/my father's lifeline
Miscellaneous: He used to be really into the drug
scene. Got arrested for being in a bar fight when he
was a bouncer—used excessive force. Judge said he
"saw something worth saving" in Toby. Said he would ex-
punge his record if he completed rehab. Toby got sober
and never went back to his old ways. Met my dad at
an AA meeting way back when—Dad was going because it was court-ordered. Gave Toby a job. He's been
with the family ever since.
Keeps my father on the straight and narrow.
Never been married. Dating Lisa seriously.
Dad doesn't know it, but I buy Toby a Father's Day
card every year, too.

We landed in London's Heathrow Airport and piled off of
the plane. Everyone was so tired. Yes, a private jet means
you're not being jammed by your tray table when the guy in
front of you leans back three inches to take a nap. But you
still feel dehydrated and achy. I looked a wreck, and I felt
like one. Cammie, of course, woke up from her sleep on the
plane looking like she'd just spent a day at the spa. Yeah, I
could hate her all right, if she weren't my best friend.

London is known for rainy weather, and sure enough,
the city didn't disappoint. After customs, we settled into
limousines and were driven to the Mandarin Oriental Hotel
in Hyde Park.

"Oh, my God! It's beautiful," Cammie murmured. It
rose majestically in the London night sky like a castle.

Toby and my father and mother were riding with us. Toby laughed. "Yeah . . . it's really nice. But you know, we used to stay someplace else. However, apparently the management didn't forget the time Greg ran through the lobby naked."

"You can walk to Harrod's, you know, girls," my father said.

I elbowed Cammie. "*She* is on a strict budget. She went through half her money in Tokyo already, Dad."

"Eh . . . toss a few things on your credit card, Livy. You girls are only going to make a trip like this once."

"Well, when Livy is a famous journalist and I'm a famous director, we'll come to London all the time," Cammie said. "We'll lunch with Charles and Camilla, the dog-faced woman. We'll be back, won't we, Liv?"

I nodded. London had a great music scene.

"Sure," Dad said. "But even if you do, you'll be older, not seventeen with no responsibilities. I wish I was your age again."

Of course, my father wasn't even responsible enough to drive a car anymore, but I didn't see the point in arguing with him. We pulled up to the hotel's lobby doors, and bell captains rushed to our cars to help us out.

George the Vampire was already processing everything. We were shown to our rooms, first passing through a glamorous lobby that seemed like it was from another era.

"I feel like a princess," Cammie whispered.

Our room was a small suite, but it was decorated elegantly in a way that made me feel as though we were transported back in time.

"Madams," the bellman said, "you have fresh flowers waiting your arrival." He swept his arm to the table, where two bouquets bloomed in huge crystal vases.

Cammie ran to them. "They're from Kai and Nick!"

My bouquet was made up of lilies. They made the whole room smell beautiful. Cammie's was an arrangement of pink roses—her favorite.

"Aren't you warming up to Kai just a little bit?" I asked after the bellboy left our bags.

"Yeah. A little. But you know, Steve and I made out in the bathroom on the plane."

"You what? When?"

"You were sleeping. We didn't do it or anything. I would have told you. But he *did* get my top off."

"Cam . . ."

"I know. But isn't it always the bad boys that girls like? You know he has a tattoo of a hypodermic needle right near his heart."

"How charming." I sighed. "I know better than to talk you out of things. Like the time you were *positive* you wanted to dye your hair pink. And the time you *swore* you would not get hurt if you got back together with Ryan. So if you're determined to make it with a bad boy—despite seeing that he is really scummy, no matter how cute he is— then make sure Operation V is at least Operation C."

She looked at me and raised one eyebrow. "What?"

"Condom. C."

"Oh. That was a given."

"Cam, can I talk to you?"

"Sure." She was already taking off her shoes and flopping down on one of the beds. "Dibs on the one closest to the bathroom."

"Fine. Look, I need to play you a tape."

"What? Let me guess. Another band I just *have* to listen to. You know, they all kind of run together. I can never tell them apart."

"Yeah, well, so do your weird French films with subtitles. No. It's not a band. You'll see. Just listen."

I dug the tape recorder out of my bag and played the Greg Essex tape. When it was over, Cammie, who had been lying down, sat up cross-legged on the bed and looked at me with tears in her eyes.

"*Your* mother?"

I nodded.

"Wow. I mean . . . you feel bad for Greg."

"I know. Listen, I'm going to go see if I can talk to my father. Nick is supposed to meet me here. He wants to take me and you out to some pubs. I'm sure Kai will come. It's harder for them here. They're really well-known in London, but he says they wear caps and go to out-of-the-way places. Anyway, if he gets here and I'm not back, just have him wait."

"What should I wear? Pink miniskirt and Bebe top? Hello Kitty T-shirt?"

"Sure, whatever. On second thought, it's rainy and feels chilly. I don't care if it is July; I'd wear jeans."

"Okay. And Liv?"

"Hmm?"

"Good luck."

"Thanks."

Paul James

a.k.a Dad

Lead singer of the Babydolls; can also play guitar—
though he says he plays badly

Best friends with Greg Essex forever, until he married
Greg's ex-girlfriend, a.k.a. Mom.

Used to do drugs. And drink. Drugs of choice: cocaine
and Valium. But mostly alcohol.

Estranged from his parents. His father died three
years ago.

Dad's been through rehab a bunch of times. Has
nearly a year sober now.

Writes all or most of the Babydolls's songs

Has to be the center of attention???? Did he keep the
band from recording Mom's songs??????

He and Mom have been together for eighteen years.
He can't do anything without her. When she was in
the hospital having her appendix out, Dad left me
with Toby and insisted on sleeping in a hospital bed
right next to Mom. Can't sleep, eat, or function without her.

I walked down the hall to the very far end and knocked on
my parents' suite. My father answered the door.

"Hey, baby."

"Hi, Dad. Where's Mom?"

"She went to the drugstore down the street. Said she
had a headache and wanted a few things. Are you two
fighting? 'Cause I just can't *stand* when she gets like this.
Crying all the time. Makes me crazy."

"Dad, we're not fighting. Well, sort of. Can I talk to you?"

"Sure."

"Okay." Suddenly I felt nervous. Did I want to find out the truth? Was there even the truth—one truth—or was Carl right?

"What, Liv? You in trouble? Drugs?"

"God, Dad. Not everyone is a fuckup."

"Watch your mouth."

I laughed. Then he did. My father had never disciplined me in my entire life. So if he said something like "Watch your mouth" or "Be in by one o'clock," we both knew I wasn't going to listen—and that I was responsible enough to take care of myself anyway. Most of the time.

"No, it's not drugs. Listen, you know how Carl is having me write stories from the road?"

My dad nodded.

"Well, he also wanted me to write about the history of the Babydolls. See, people your age—decrepit, you know—"

"Very funny."

"*Ancient* people like you know the whole story. But kids *my* age only know you now because your song was used in the movie and all of a sudden you're getting tons of airplay. Plus the boxed set was released. You're a big deal now. But they don't know the whole story of your roots and how huge you were. Not to mention the breakup."

"Okay. I got you."

"So I interviewed Greg, Dad."

"Why?"

I sighed. It seemed obvious to me. "Because he's the lead guitarist. Became James and Essex wrote some of the

107

world's most famous rock songs. Because he's a friggin' *Babydoll*."

"He's also an asshole," Dad said a little flatly.

"Here's the thing, Dad. He doesn't see it that way."

"Assholes usually don't."

"He says he tried to shoot you because you never would have let Mom be as famous as you. That she was an incredible songwriter and you wouldn't record her songs. He said he slit his wrists for her."

My father looked at me intensely. He took a deep breath, and then he said, "I'm not going to talk to you about this. It's none of your business." He began pacing nervously, absentmindedly touching the crystal he wore on a velvet cord around his neck.

"It *is* my business."

"No, Liv. I love you, but all of that is private."

"No. It's not. It's the gossip and innuendo that has swirled around our family and the Babydolls since before I was even born. Whether you like it or not, Dad . . . whatever happened in Paris that night is part of me, too. You raised me in this rock-and-roll world—and I think I deserve to know the truth. What happened?"

"I don't remember."

"Dad . . . don't do that. Look, you've been interviewed a thousand times about that night. And everyone says he was just jealous you married Mom. And you stole her away from him. But I think there's more to it." He was still pacing, and I went and stood in front of him.

"You talk to Greg one day, one interview, and you doubt me, Liv? That hurts. Just stab me, why don't you?"

"God, you're all a bunch of drama queens!"

"Look . . . I've screwed up every which way that's possible. There are rehabs with brass plaques on the door to my room, I've been so often. I was too messed up to even read you bedtime stories most nights. But I've been trying real hard, Livy. You can't take that away from me. And it's been *hard*."

"I know, Dad." I softened.

"No. You don't. Thank *God* you don't seem to have inherited any of my problems, Liv. You don't know what it's like to kiss your daughter good-night, kiss your beautiful wife good night, go to bed, and wake up at three o'clock in the morning and not be able to sleep because you just want a drink *so bad* that you feel like you're going to have a nervous breakdown. You'd do anything to score drugs. I've earned this sobriety day by day, hour by hour, and sometimes minute by minute. And I'm not going to go back in time to when someone tried to fucking *shoot* me, and defend my love for your mother."

I'd heard my father talk like that before. He was always the one who avoided heavy talks. He couldn't discipline me, and he couldn't handle anything "heavy." That was just the way he was.

"Okay, Dad. I'm sorry."

"Does Greg think he's the only one who loved her? I watched your mother curl into the fetal position and cry like I'd never seen a person cry before over that jerk. I watched her watch him as he walked off with some groupies to cheat on her. He killed her a little bit each day. I'm no prize, Liv, but he's not the knight in shining armor he's pretending to be for you."

We looked at each other. My eyes were so much like his. Identical. I threw my arms around his neck. "Okay."

He hugged me back, really hard. Then he changed the subject. "Enough heavy stuff. What are you and Cammie doing tonight?"

"Pub crawling with Nick and Kai."

"Be home by two."

"Yeah, right."

"See, I don't get it. Other fathers say things like that and their kids listen."

"No, they don't. The parents just *think* they listen."

"And for the record?"

"Yeah?"

"Your mom's going insane that you're seeing Nick. But I like him. He's cool in my book."

"Thanks."

I turned and left my parents' room. I realized that the truth was a lot like rock and roll: It meant different things to different people, just like when I heard "Black Hole Sun" I left my body briefly, and for Cammie, it was just another dumb song.

Chapter Sixteen

Back in our room, Cammie and I finished unpacking and getting ready. My hair was reacting to the London dampness already by curling on the ends.

Cammie and I stood side by side in the bathroom, fixing our makeup. I didn't bring all that much with me. I use MAC and have blush, powder, mascara, gloss, and eyeliner. One of each. One cleanser. One moisturizer. I have more at home, but I knew Cammie would bring a *trunk* of makeup, so I figured why bother bringing mine when I'd be on the road with a makeup diva?

"So how did it go?"

"How does it ever go when I try to have a serious discussion with Paul James?"

"Not well."

"Actually, he really did talk to me, but you know, there are three different ways of looking at the whole thing. I still have to interview my mom—and Steve Zane. I think I should even interview George the Vampire. And Toby."

Someone knocked on our door.

"That's him!" I squealed. Then I stopped.

"What?"

"My voice. Did you just hear me?"

"Yes. Livy James has officially gone crazy over a *rock*

111

god. Despite seventeen years of saying she would never date a musician."

"Well, technically I've only been saying that since I was twelve."

I walked out of the bathroom, checked myself in the mirror over the dresser one last time, and then went to open the door.

"Livy!" Nick grabbed me around my waist and pulled me tight to him. He had this way, when he kissed me, of biting my lower lip a little—very sexy.

"Don't mind me," Kai joked, and walked around us to go give Cammie a kiss on the cheek.

"Thanks for the flowers," she said.

"You like the color?"

She nodded.

"I had to guess by all the pink you wear."

"Livy's the black-wearing rock and roller. Me, I like hot pink."

Nick and I pulled away from each other. How could I miss someone so much whom I just had seen two days ago? Or was it one day ago? I was losing track of time and time zones. I didn't even know what *day* it was in London.

"Come on! The best pubs in London are awaiting us."

We left our room and took the elevator down to the lobby. Outside the hotel, Nick had the doorman hail us a cab. We climbed in. I sat on Nick's lap, and Kai and Cammie sat next to us.

"No limo tonight," Kai said. "We'll look like wankers pullin' up in front of a pub in one."

The cabbie looked in the rearview mirror. "Where to?"

"Red Lion Pub. Know it?"

The cabbie nodded. He pulled into traffic, but as he drove, he kept glancing in the rearview mirror. "Hey . . . you're the guys from the Wolves. 'Head in the Clouds' and all that. Right?"

I turned to look at Kai and then at Nick. I hadn't even noticed really. Their version of a disguise meant they were wearing ball caps turned 'round backward, and they hadn't shaved. Kai had his shirt collar turned up.

"You got us, mate," Kai said. "Look . . . how 'bout we make you a deal?"

"What kind of deal?"

"What's your name?"

"Sid." Our cabbie looked about twenty-five, with reddish hair and pale skin, and he had four earrings in his left ear. He had a bobblehead of Prince Charles on his dashboard next to a bobblehead of Elvis.

"Okay, Sid," Kai said. "We want a night out with our girls without being troubled. So how's about we hire your cab for the night? The meter can run . . . and if we're in a pub and suddenly it starts getting dodgy and people bug us for autographs, we just pay our tab and dash off and you'll be waiting. You be our chariot for the night."

"Sure."

"Great. And when we're done, we'll sign anything you want, and take your address and send you some CDs, okay?" Nick said.

"Deal."

Sid drove us to the first pub, and I had my first taste of British lager. It was enough to make me throw up. I don't like *American* beer, let alone *warm* British beer. But Kai and Nick showed us how to play darts, and we watched soccer on the television and cheered when the entire pub cheered. Then two girls noticed Nick, and we were mobbed by people wanting to buy us rounds and talk to them about the tour. It was a big deal that they were appearing on their home turf. All my life I had to share my father with strangers. Even at my ninth birthday party, parents of my friends made fools of themselves. Some brought CDs for him to sign. I hated our world being intruded on, but Nick and Kai were polite. Soon we made a dash toward the door and we were off to the next pub, and then the next one.

I stopped at my third lager. I didn't even finish the first two. Cammie and Kai and Nick, though, were really pounding them down. Sometime around one o'clock, last call was given, and we went out to Sid's cab. Kai was singing "Hey Jude" by the Beatles at the top of his lungs. Sid was amused. He drove us back to our hotel, and Kai and Cammie got out and decided they were going to walk around the block—Kai said he wanted some fresh air. Nick tipped Sid two hundred dollars, and Nick and I went into the lobby.

"Come up to my room? Just mine. I don't share it like you and Cammie," he whispered in my ear, tickling me so that the hair on my neck prickled.

"I don't know." I could see he was drunk.

"Please?" He nibbled on my neck, and I agreed. He was so hard to say no to.

We rode up in the elevator and went to his suite. As soon as we were inside, he was all over me.

"Nick . . . please stop."

"Why?" He had his hand up my shirt.

"Nick . . . look . . . I . . ."

He kissed me harder and maneuvered me to his bed. We lay down together, almost falling, kissing.

"Wait!"

"What, Livy? Don't you know I'm crazy about you?" He took off his shirt, and I could see his other tattoo, the one on his stomach. It was right where a delicate line of soft hair traced its way from his belly button. He was beautiful.

"What does that tattoo mean?"

"Symbol for paradise."

I smiled. "Kind of cocky, aren't you?" I teased.

"No. I just tell it like it is." He laughed.

"Nick, you know I'm younger than you are, right?"

"I know."

"Well . . . I . . . haven't done it."

"That's okay." He ran his hand through my hair. "I swear I'll be good to you, Liv."

"It's not just that. I grew up in this really crazy world, and if I was going to do it with you, if you were going to be my first, it wouldn't be when you were drunk."

"What does that mean? We were having a good time tonight." His voice was edgy.

"It means you're drunk, and that's fine, but it's not what I want to do when you're drunk."

"Liv, I'm not your da. I'm my own person."

"And I'm not one of these girls who's just going to sleep with you without even thinking about it. Without it meaning anything."

He sat up. "Is that what you think? That you don't mean anything to me?" His eyes were glassy. It reminded me of arguing with my father when he used to have a few.

"No. I know I mean something to you. I'd just mean more if you were sober right now."

"Fook it. I don't need this, Liv. I think I've proven myself to you."

Now I was pissed. I rolled over and climbed off the bed and stood up. "Proven yourself to me? *Proven* yourself to me? Why? Because you decided to spend time with me? Big-time rock star hanging out with some high school girl? Because you took me to a temple and showed me around Tokyo? That's proof?"

I thought of Greg slitting his wrists for my mother. Love made people do crazy things, but Nick had proven nothing. Not to me.

"I think of you all the time, Livy. I've shown you that you're special to me. It's not like I grabbed you backstage for a fast one. This means something."

"Not to me. Not now."

I turned and, fighting tears, stormed out of his room and slammed the door, running down the hall to the elevators.

There it was. His rock-and-roll ego was as big as my father's.

Chapter Seventeen

"Sympathy for the Devil"
                    —The Rolling Stones

He didn't come chasing after me. Or he might have, but I ran down the hall to the elevator and didn't look back. I took it down to my floor and went to my room. I pressed my ear up against the door and could hear the television on and Cammie's voice—and Kai's. I didn't want to bother them, and I didn't want to talk about what happened. I felt like someone had stabbed me. And it was my own stupid fault. I broke my own rule, and look what it got me.

Well, for one thing, it got me nowhere to sleep.

If I went to my parents' room, my mother would give me a big, fat "I told you so."

So I decided to go to Toby's room. I started to walk down the hall, when the elevator doors opened. I turned around, expecting Nick, but it was Steve Zane. He gave me a wave.

"Hey, Liv. You're out here late."

I shrugged. I didn't trust my voice, and the *last* thing I wanted to do was start crying in front of him.

"Wait up. . . ." He walked faster down the hall.

I took a deep breath.

I will not cry.

I will not cry.

117

I will not cry.

I will not cry.

Olivia Melody James . . . Do not cry!

"Hey . . ." He caught up with me. "You look like you lost your best friend. Where's Cam?"

"Oh . . ." My voice quavered. "She . . . um . . ." And then I lost it. "Shit!" I snapped as tears started rolling down my face. My throat felt so tight, and then a sob came up from somewhere. *Great.* In front of Steve Zane. That was like crying in front of Satan. I shook my head. Could the night be any more of a disaster?

"Hey . . ." He shushed me and gave me a hug. "Come on . . . come on, don't cry. What's wrong? Do you want me to go get your father?"

"Oh . . . God . . . no . . . anything but that."

"Come on then." He put his arm around my shoulders and started steering me toward his hotel suite. I had visions of having to fend *him* off now. Wonderful. Now I would be alone with the man who liked to show girls what was on his penis. Rumor has it he had a spider tattooed there.

"Look, Steve." I sniffled when we got to his door. "I'll be fine. I'm just going to go take a walk."

He inserted his electronic key card into the door slot. "Over my dead body. This is a major city, and you're not going anywhere alone. Everyone can think I'm the irresponsible one—and that's saying a lot, compared to the rest of the band—but I'm not letting you go out alone."

"Well, I have nowhere to go right now."

"Cammie with someone?"

I nodded.

He ushered me into his suite. "Is that why you're upset?"

"No, it's not that. Hold on. . . ." I went into the bathroom, turned on the light, and washed my face a bit and blew my nose. I came back out. Steve had cracked open a cold beer from the minibar.

"Sit down." He gestured to the couch next to him. I opted for a chair on the *other* side of the coffee table.

He laughed. "I promise you I won't bite."

I smiled. "Good. Now that we have that out of the way . . ."

"Want a beer or something? Diet Coke?"

"I'll take a soda." I got up and walked to the minibar and got a diet Coke, opened it, and drank from the can.

"So you want to tell me what happened?"

"Not really."

"Bet you'd feel better if you did."

"Well . . ." I bit my lip. "I don't know."

"Liv . . . I promise you, I'll be a good boy and just listen. Swear it."

"I . . . well . . . Nick Hoffman and I hooked up. I didn't want to."

"What? The bastard forced himself on you?" Steve leaned forward.

"No, no. Nothing like that. Look, I have a rule, a motto: No musicians. Period. I never, ever wanted to be involved with one. Ever. Did I mention never, ever?"

Steve nodded. "We screwed you up good, didn't we?"

"What do you mean?"

"I mean, if you hadn't grown up around us—and all the

wild stuff we've done—you never would have that rule. You must hate us."

"I don't hate you. I . . . well, I just had that rule. But then I met Nick . . . and the rule sort of flew out the window. I mean, I really, *really* liked him."

"Got it. Okay. And what's the problem?"

"The problem is that in Tokyo, he was so romantic and sweet, and we got close really fast, and it was intense. We would go out for lunch or spend time together and never run out of things to say. And he was on his best behavior in Tokyo."

"What's that supposed to mean?"

"It means he was perfect. *Too* perfect. Then we got to London, and he's from London, so he was all excited to show me the city. He and Kai took Cammie and me around to some pubs. He got drunk and . . ."

"Let me guess. He made a total fucking asshole of himself."

"Pretty much. He was pushing for . . . you know . . . too much, and it wasn't that I didn't think I *might* want to someday do it with him, but the point is that it sure as hell wouldn't be while he was drunk."

"I hear you, Liv."

I looked over at Steve. "How come you're so . . . Forget it."

"No. Say what you were going to say."

"Well, so nice. Or understanding. I mean, you *are* the guy I saw doing breast shots a couple of nights ago."

He laughed and took a swig of his beer. "Look, I'm a bad boy. I admit it. But put yourself in my shoes. If you like sex, and you like drugs, and you like booze, and people throw all of the above at you—with no effort whatsoever on your part—why would you turn it down?"

"I don't know. I hear you, but I guess it's just not my scene, so . . ."

"Well, it's always been my scene. Think about it, Livy. I was just an underage bass player in rat-hole clubs in New York City, and I started playing with these older guys—The Babydolls. I was introduced to some scary stuff, and I was a baby-faced fifteen-year-old. It's no wonder I fell into this life. It was thrown at me when I was too young to handle it. I've tried to settle down a little bit here and there. I stopped doing heroin because I just couldn't function on it. But in the end, Liv, I'm a bad boy."

"Yeah, you are," I said, grinning a little.

"But that doesn't mean I'm *total* scum. I do care about people who are important to me. Liv, I've known you since the day you were born. We were all a lot closer then, and I held you in the damn hospital. Your father had paid for this special suite—like a hotel. It was a VIP suite right at the hospital. And he paid for it, had it filled with flowers, and we all hung out in there. Not Greg, but the rest of us."

"You guys are all sort of this extended family to me. That's why I wish everyone could get along. I don't know. . . . I'm so confused about the Babydolls, about Nick. Thanks for listening, Steve."

"Liv?"

"Yeah?"

"For the record, I never would have banged Cammie."

"Why not? You don't think she's pretty?"

"She's friggin' beautiful. And we fooled around. But like I said, I may be a bad boy, but I don't relish the idea of you looking at me like I'm a fuckin' male whore for the rest of my life—any more than you do now, of course. I wouldn't have gone all the way with her."

"Anyone ever tell you how complicated you are?"

"Yeah. Your mother used to tell me that. She was like a big sister to me."

"Steve . . . were you there that night?"

"Paris?"

"Yeah."

Steve leaned his head back against the couch and sighed. Then he looked straight at me. "I was there."

"So what do you think happened?"

"Greg shot at your father. Your father tried to strangle him. Then they tried to wrestle each other off the balcony. Just another night with the Babydolls." He grinned and winked at me.

"That's not what I mean. . . . I want to know what you think happened. *Why* it happened. What made them fight like that? I mean, they'd fought before, but to try to kill each other?"

Steve took another huge swig of beer and emptied the bottle. He stood, crossed the room, and got another beer.

"Well, Greg and your father both were in love with your mother. And I really think . . . I mean, what I say stays in this room. Deal?" He sat back down.

"Deal."

"Okay. Your mother had married your father, but she and Greg never stopped talking to each other. I mean, nothing was going on. They weren't sleeping together, so get that idea out of your head. She was pregnant with you, for God's sake. But if she fought with your dad, then she called Greg and they would talk for hours. I think she still loved Greg. And I think your father found out about that, and one thing led to another and they tried to kill each other."

"Yet another version of the infamous night in Paris."

"What do you mean?"

"Everyone has a different story of what really happened."

"Yeah, well, stick all four Babydolls in a room and you'll never get us to agree."

I yawned. "My brain hurts. Thinking about Nick. Thinking about the Babydolls."

"You want my advice?"

"I can't believe I'm asking for advice from the bad boy of the Babydolls, but sure."

"I've been around some of the wildest, sleaziest men in the music biz. I've seen some pretty sketchy things. Hey, who am I kidding? I've *participated* in some very sketchy things. And you know that expression 'It takes one to know one'?"

"Yeah."

"Well, Nick Hoffman ain't a bad boy, Liv. He couldn't be one if he tried. You know, when it came time to work out the tour, the only thing that stupid kid thought about was if we could coordinate food drives for the food banks, and all his karma shit. Enough to make a guy like me nauseous."

I sort of half smiled.

"Chin up, Liv. I mean it. And I know I'll seem like a pig for saying this, but you are beautiful. I'm sure he just had a little too much to drink and was an ass. But he didn't mean anything by it."

"Maybe he did. Maybe he didn't."

"Don't be a 'fraidy cat."

"What's that supposed to mean?"

"Look, take it from a guy who's lived enough for ten people . . . you're how old?"

"Seventeen. Just turned seventeen."

"And you're heading into some of the best years, Liv. College—not that I went, but we've *played* a college or two. Good parties."

I smiled. "You ever think about anything else?"

"Besides partying and sex? Not really. But I have packed a lot of living into my life. And you can't be afraid, Liv."

"What do you mean?"

"You can't be so afraid of getting hurt that you miss what the world has to offer. Because guess what?"

"What?"

"You will get hurt. You will get hurt so bad it will feel like you won't survive it. And that's part of life. So if you really dig Nick Hoffman—and I can see the connection between you—if you really like him that much, you should stop being afraid. Put your heart out there and take a chance."

"Anyone ever tell you that for someone so screwed up, you make a lot of sense?"

"No one ever tells me that. You know why?"

I shook my head.

" 'Cause everyone assumes I'm too much of a screwup to actually have any insight. But sometimes it's guys like me that know more about living than all the rest of you."

"Thanks, Steve." I yawned. "I've got to go find a place to crash. I'm going to go wake up Toby."

"Gimme a break, Liv. Sleep here. You take my bed. I'll take the couch."

"No . . . I can't do that."

"Look, I pop four Valium to sleep anyway. In fifteen minutes I wouldn't know if a bomb exploded in here. So crash in my bed. Don't insult me by thinking you can't trust me."

He looked straight at me, and I couldn't say no. He was right. He had been really decent tonight.

"Okay, Steve." I stood up and walked over to him and kissed him on the cheek. "Thanks a lot."

"Anytime."

True to his word, he went into the bathroom, took four Valium washed down with another beer, and was passed out in ten minutes. I kept my clothes on and slid under the sheets. I felt emotionally drained and was asleep just a few minutes after Steve was.

Chapter Eighteen

The next morning I woke up and looked at the clock radio. Nine o'clock. I didn't expect anyone to be up, but I figured I could at least go back to my room quietly and shower. I also wanted to get my laptop. I needed to write. I *longed* to write. Writing always helped me make sense of everything in my life.

I climbed out of bed and went to the desk. Opening the top drawer, I found, like in most expensive hotels, fancy linen-paper stationery and a pen. I wrote a note to leave for Steve.

> *Dear Steve,*
>
> *Thanks for everything—listening, the advice, the place to crash. I learned that sometimes things aren't what they seem. Sometimes people are a lot more than they seem. Thanks for looking out for me.*
>
> *Love,*
> *Livy*

I took the note and left it on the coffee table. Steve was sleeping in the most uncomfortable-looking position on the couch, but he was out cold. I bent down and kissed his cheek, then took the comforter from the bed and put it over him. Sleeping, he didn't look like one of the baddest wild men in rock and roll. He just looked like a boy—a sleeping little boy. Part of me wished that he would get sober like my dad and Charlie, and maybe stop doing some of the things he did. But I also knew that wishing people would change doesn't make them change. I thought of AA's Serenity Prayer:

> *God, grant me the serenity to accept the things I*
> *cannot change,*
> *The courage to change the things I can,*
> *And the wisdom to know the difference.*

I don't know if I was wise, but I did know Steve was firmly set in his ways.

I went out into the hall. Looking down toward my room, I saw Nick sitting on the floor, leaning up against the wall. I had no idea what to say to him.

But I didn't have to worry—because he was on the attack.

"Where were you?"

I didn't answer.

"I asked you a question, Liv. You storm out of my room like a high school girl and disappear—and now I see you coming out of someone else's room in the morning. Whose room is that?"

I gave him a dirty look. "None of your business."

"Fine. I'll go knock on the bloody door."

"No one will answer. It's Steve Zane's room. He's passed out."

"I don't believe this."

"Get over yourself, Nick. Cammie and Kai were in my room, and I had nowhere to crash."

"So you picked *him*? This is a big hotel . . . you couldn't have gotten another room?"

"Not when I was crying at two o'clock in the morning."

He stood up. "I came to find you. I slept here all night."

"Why? Why did you come to find me?"

"Forget it. Hope you're very happy with Steve. What a load of shit you fed me. You don't trust me, but you trust *him?*"

The door to my room opened, and Cammie peered her head out. She was wearing her Hello Kitty robe—and, as usual, looked perfect. I felt my hair. As usual first thing when I woke up, it felt like a Brillo pad.

"What's going on?" Her voice was sleepy.

"Nothing," I said. "I just need to come in and shower."

"She spent the night with Steve Zane last night. I guess she calls that nothing. I'm outta here." Nick stormed off.

"Not fast enough," I muttered, and walked past Cam and into my room. Kai was pulling on his jeans.

"Is Nick okay?"

Cammie had shut the door and was looking at me—but not the way Nick did, accusingly. She was looking at me waiting, expectantly. She knew there had to be a story behind it, and she would wait until I told her.

"I don't care if Nick's okay."

Cam came over and rubbed my back. "What happened?"

"He was pretty drunk last night and started assuming a few things. You know how I feel about him, but he was drunk, and it was a little too soon. I left his room, and then you two were in here. So I went out in the hall, and I was crying and just a mess. Steve was just getting in from Lord knows where. He wouldn't let me be alone. Was all worried. I went into his room with him, and we talked—just talked. He *defended* Nick—though I can see now Nick didn't deserve it. He gave me his bed, and he slept on the couch and didn't lay a hand on me. I left this morning. The rest . . . you saw."

"I'll talk to him," Kai said, pulling his shirt on over his head.

"Don't bother."

I felt like I was going to cry again, so I walked in the bathroom, shut the door, and took a piping-hot shower. I have never been the type of person to cry over things. But from feeling blissfully happy in Tokyo to feeling the pits of despair in rainy England was enough to make me want to go to bed, crawl under the covers, watch movies on television, and eat a pint of ice cream. Mint chocolate chip, to be exact.

Every once in while, when Cammie and I have PMS at the same time, we stay in our pj's all day and watch rented movies and eat a ton of junk food. She's partial to popcorn with *lots* of butter. And salt. Washed down with diet Dr Pepper.

I stayed in the shower until my fingers looked like prunes, turned off the water and dried off with the hotel's fluffy towels, then put on my robe. I went back out in the bedroom. Kai had left while I was in the shower, and Cam came over to me and gave me a huge hug.

"I'm so sorry, Liv. I didn't plan on Kai being here. I really didn't. If it wasn't for that, you never would have ended up in Steve's room, and this whole misunderstanding never would have happened."

"Cam." I pulled away and flopped on my bed. "If he liked me half as much as he said he did, he would *know* that this is a misunderstanding."

"You know guys when their egos are bruised. He'll realize he's being a jerk."

"I don't care one way or the other."

"Yes, you do. But . . . for now we'll say you don't."

"Enough about my mess of a love life for a while. What happened with you and Kai?"

"You know, Liv, I think Operation V would be just as successful with Kai as Steve Zane."

"I told you that having it *mean* something—with someone nice—would be better. So you didn't, did you?"

"No. We didn't. But we fooled around, and I think we might. Do you know he's really into films, too? I talked to him about film school. Both of us really love the same directors. Scorsese . . . Kai's a Buddhist, like Nick. *Kundun* was his favorite movie. And I love the imagery in that film."

When Cam got to talking about film, it was like how I felt talking about music. She noticed amazing details and could talk about her favorite movies until I wanted to strangle her. But just like she listened to me discuss Jane's Addiction and Perry Farrell and, well, just about all my favorite bands, I put up with her love of film. Even the foreign ones I thought no one in their right mind liked.

"I'm happy for you, Cam," I said, rolling over on my side and leaning up on my elbow.

"And I'm sad for you. But I just *know* it's going to work out. Kai says you're all Nick talks about. Did you know Nick liked you before he even met you?"

"Huh?"

"Well, not liked, but he thought you were beautiful. He saw a picture of you and your father taken at the MTV Video Music Awards last year."

"Really?"

"Uh-huh. And he showed your picture to Kai. It was on a fan Web site somewhere for the Babydolls. Anyway, I bet right now he's feeling awful."

"If there really *is* such a thing as karma, he is!"

"Now stop, Liv. What are we going to do today before the concert?"

"Toby said he would go with us to the wax museum, and the Tower of London . . . and, God help me for the word leaving my mouth—Harrod's."

"Only the most famous department store in the world."

"I knew I would regret it."

"You're still going to the concert tonight, right?"

I nodded. "When we get back from shopping, I want to interview my mom. Then we'll go to the concert. Tomorrow we leave for my grandparents' house."

"I still don't get why they don't talk to your mom much."

"Neither do I. But she left home at eighteen to sing with a band, and my grandfather is a professor of music. I don't think he likes rock and roll."

131

"Will you be upset if I don't go with you to their house?"

"No, why?"

"Well . . . Kai and I have a romantic night planned after the concert tomorrow. We're going to go to the Millennium Bridge and toss a penny and make a wish, and then come back here for champagne. And . . . perhaps my summer Operation V will be a success tomorrow night."

"I'm just relieved it's Kai and not Steve Zane."

"Did Steve Zane really not lay a hand on you?"

I nodded. "Swear. He's screwed up—don't get me wrong. But underneath that bad-boy image is someone different. In a Steve Zane kind of way."

Cammie and I got dressed and packed our backpacks for the day of sightseeing. Just as we were about to walk out the door, our phone rang. I picked it up and heard Nick say, "Livy, please listen—"

But I hung up the phone before he could finish the sentence.

Now more than ever, I believed in "no musicians."

Chapter Nineteen

"It's My Life"
—No Doubt

Cammie in Harrod's was scary. Toby and I followed her around, making her put items back on the shelves and racks. It's not that I didn't want her to have a good time and buy some things, but Cammie, when she's excited about shopping, will buy what she doesn't need. Only *later,* when she's broke, will she look at her purchases and say, "What was I thinking? I don't even ski, so why did I buy this ski jacket?"

We had a great time, the three of us. We helped Toby pick out gifts for Lisa. He called her twice from his cell phone while we were out. I even heard him say, "I love you." Which for Toby was a really big deal.

Shopping helped me keep my mind off of Nick. Well, not really. I still thought about him every other second, but being out was a nice distraction. After shopping, we returned to our hotel. My feet hurt—we'd done the museum and, even in sneakers, I felt like I walked miles. When Cammie and I got to our room we found dozens of roses.

"They're from Nick," Cammie said. "Look at them all. They must have cost a fortune!"

"Well, then he wasted his money."

I put down my shopping bag—I'd bought a pretty blue cashmere sweater that Cammie *swore* matched the color of my eyes. Grabbing my backback, I said, "Back in a bit. Going to go try to get my mom on tape."

"Good luck, Liv. And be nice to her."

"What's that supposed to mean?"

"You heard the tape from Greg. None of it sounds like it was easy for her. I'm glad I never had a guy go that nuts over me."

I stopped for a minute. "Me, too," I whispered and shut the door and walked down to my parents' suite and knocked.

Anna James
Wife of Paul James, a.k.a., my mother
Even Mick Jagger says she was the prettiest woman in London when she was nineteen. She left home early to try to break into the music business. Sang. Wrote songs (according to Greg). She fell in love with Greg Essex. What happened???
Married my dad. I came along. Was a good mom, but it was like she had two kids—me and Dad.
Very artistic. Designs all my shirts. Paints. Gardens. Like she's channeling all her talent into making things.

My mom answered the door. "Liv? God . . . I feel like I lose track of you when we're on tour. Come in and tell me what you've been up to. What did you and Cammie do today? Or was it you and Nick?"

"Me, Cammie, and Toby. He and I tried to prevent Cammie from ODing on shopping. We went to the Tower of London and did some other sightseeing."

"Great. Did you have a good time?"

I nodded. "Where's Dad?"

"Radio station. Then he has an appearance at a record store, autographing CDs. Long day. He'll be tired tonight. They all will be."

"Mom? Can I interview you? For my article." I took out the tape recorder.

"Oh, I don't know that I'm terribly important to the story, Liv."

"Mom, you are. You heard Greg's tape. *You're* as much a part of the Babydolls' history as all of them."

"It's all so long ago, Liv. And some of it I'd rather leave in the past."

"*Please,* Mom?"

She sighed. After a minute, she said, "All right. But only because I love you."

She sat down in a chair, and I pressed record and put it on the table, then sat opposite her.

"How did you meet the Babydolls?"

She smiled. "God, it's been *forever.* This makes me feel *old.* I had left home. Didn't get along with my mum and dad—still don't, as you know—it's why I hate fighting with you. I don't want to push you away. Anyway, I started hanging out in clubs in London, and it was just a time when new music was coming out of the London scene. I mean, British rock has always influenced the rest of the world—the Beatles, the Stones, New Wave, punk. I had a rather good voice. An alright voice. I started meeting singers looking for background vocalists. I recorded a duet with Jimmy Jameson— he was a one-hit wonder. And eventually, I met Greg."

"Was it love at first sight?"

"Oh, don't tell your dad this, but yes. Greg was an *amazing* guitarist, and he had a lovely voice himself. He wanted me to come check out his band, the Babydolls. Now, I'd heard of them. Everyone had heard of them . . . that they would be the next big thing from America, that sort of buzz. I saw them play in a club, and I was stunned. Your father, Liv, made a room go electric. He was what they call a rock god. And when they got a huge record deal and a big touring opportunity, I went along as a backup singer and Greg's girlfriend."

"Why did you two break up?"

"Liv, it's terribly complicated. You know, I was no angel. I really wasn't. None of us were. Drugs, drinking, partying. It was a wild time. Wilder when the world is literally throwing stuff at your feet. But Greg, he got into heroin. Dabbled in it. He wasn't a full-blown addict, but he was terribly messed up. And when he was on drugs, he'd do horrible things, like betray me with other women and so on."

Her voice grew softer, and I had to tell her to speak up a bit. "Just your normal speaking voice, okay, Mom?"

She nodded.

"So how did you end up with Dad?"

"I suppose there wasn't a girl in the world who wasn't in love with him a little bit, Liv. It was how he was onstage. Actually, it wasn't *just* how he was when he was performing; it was where he took you."

"What do you mean?"

"He took people outside of themselves—they felt part

of this experience, part of the music. I was so in awe of his talent. And when I was feeling hurt, feeling lonely, he listened to me."

"And so what happened?"

"I just made a decision."

"A decision?"

She nodded. "I knew I could feel like my insides were ripped out over and over again with Greg. That it would be intense—both the good and the bad. When I was apart from him, I felt ill. But when he was acting crazy, it nearly destroyed me. I began to think that I could have a quieter kind of love with your father. Still very beautiful—but a different kind of love. Does that make sense? Your father loved me in a way that wouldn't destroy us both."

I was quiet. After a few seconds, I nodded. "Yeah. But what did you think when Greg slit his wrists?"

"Just because someone loves you obsessively, Livy, doesn't mean that you owe it to him to jump into that obsession with him. When you're young, you think that kind of crazy love is exciting, but when you grow up a bit, you realize it's like an illness, a sickness."

"And what about Greg's tape? What about the night in Paris?"

"The infamous night in Paris."

I nodded. "What really happened that night?"

She looked away and bit her lip; then she looked off into the distance a bit, as if remembering the night. "After I married your father, tensions into the band kept mounting. Pressures from the media. They were calling me the Yoko Ono of the Babydolls. I got hate mail. People thought

I was terrible for dumping Greg for your father—only they really had no idea what I had been through. You were born, and I hoped it would settle your father down a bit more. Greg and he were best friends, and I could see, every day, the strain between them growing. But I was in those first months of baby love. And I was tired of touring, tired of the groupies hanging around, and tired, honestly, of sharing your father with the rest of the world. I wanted it to just be the three of us."

"Dad loves attention, though."

"I know," she said sadly. "But I was hoping in my heart that he would grow up. Anyway, we were all in Paris, and Greg was tormenting your poor father. He had been doing drugs. I think they both had. And Greg started saying, 'How does it feel, Paul, to know she'll never love you the way she loves me?' "

"How awful."

"Oh, it got worse from there. When I broke up with Greg, I *did* tell him I loved him in a way I would never love anyone else. That was true. It remains true. But I also believed he would never get well, and I wasn't going to spend the rest of my life watching him commit slow suicide. But he just kept throwing it in your father's face. Then Greg said that he thought you were his."

I felt all the color leave my face. "I'm not, though, right?"

"Oh, Liv, my love, no. Of course not. But your father just lost it. He told Greg that I would never forgive all the whores he'd slept with, that I felt *sorry* for him, that I found his drug abuse weak, a character flaw. They started hurling all these vicious insults at each other. And Greg took out a gun and tried to shoot your father."

"But what about all he says on the tape, about your talent, your songwriting, your singing? About Dad only being able to handle one star in the family?"

"Maybe the person who can only handle one star in the family is me, Livy."

"What do you mean?"

"It means, if I had really wanted to be like the Baby-dolls—to not be able to walk down the street without being mobbed—I'm pretty sure Greg is right. I could have made it."

"So why didn't you?"

"Because I had a front-row seat for the way you have to sell your soul to the devil for fame. Your father loves walking into a restaurant and instantly being given the best table. He loves signing autographs, being on MTV, and pretty much having no privacy except in our own home. When he's had to go to rehab, people have *sold* that story to the highest bidder—orderlies from the hospitals, caseworkers, whatever. They're like vultures. That's not what I wanted."

"So you never regretted not being famous in your own right?"

"Oh, Liv, there's no one, darling, without regrets."

"What about me? Do you regret me?"

"Never. Not for a moment. I regret that your father is a little like a child himself. That I have to take care of him, so sometimes you seem to get the short end of things. I regret . . . Forget it."

"No, tell me."

"I regret that I never wanted the kind of fame your father and Greg and Charlie and Steve have. I would have loved to have had some of my songs recorded. I loved writing music. But my life is fine the way it is, Liv." She paused a minute. "Now it's my turn to ask you a question: Do you regret having us for parents? Sometimes I feel like we've made a total mess of things."

"Sometimes I hate it. But then when I go to Cam's house and see what it's like in a 'normal' household, I'm not sure I'd like that any better."

"Liv, I'm sorry about telling you to be careful with Nick Hoffman. As a parent, you want your child to avoid the same mistakes you made when you were young. I think you have so much to offer the world as a writer, I just don't want you to get sidetracked the way I did."

I turned off the tape recorder. "I don't think it's going to work out between Nick and me. When I'm with him, I feel like . . . I just feel like there's no one else in the world. But I really think the whole rock scene just makes relationships impossible."

"Well, I can't believe I'm saying this, but it does depend on the person, Liv."

"I know."

"You're still going to the concert tonight, though, right?"

"Yeah. I have to write about it. Then tomorrow Cam's going to stay and I'm going to go to Grandma and Grandpa's. Are you sure you won't come?"

"I'm sure. Trust me, it's you they want to see."

"I still don't understand why you don't get along with them."

"Oh, I suppose it's just ancient hurts from so many years ago. It's like we all carry with us old scars that can't seem to heal."

I stood up and kissed her on the cheek. "I'm sorry for fighting, Mom."

"I'm sorry for not realizing how grown-up you are. You'll figure it all out."

"I hope so, Mom. I really hope so."

Chapter Twenty

"Lipstick Sunset"
—John Hiatt

TO: Carl Erikson
CC: Rob Hernandez
FR: Livy James
RE: Postcard from London/attachment

Hi, Carl.

Attached you'll find a few pictures from Wembley Stadium. Most of them are of my father. One is of Nick Hoffman leaping into the crowd. Here's what I wrote to go along with it.

> *They say you can never go home again. But the Wolves proved them wrong last night at Wembley Stadium. The Wolves have a huge following here, and even their new material drew screams from the crowd as sun set over England.*

> *Then, the Babydolls took to the stage. Behind them, on giant screens, was a montage of footage from concerts past. They've changed. Paul James looks the most like his twenty-*

year-old self. Charlie Hopper has traded in his long locks for a goatee and nearly shaved head. Greg Essex and Steve Zane have cut their hair, too, and they look more mature. Their sound, if possible, is tighter. But the most amazing element is watching kids who were too young to have appreciated the band when they first exploded from the music scene, so into it they act as if they're the generation to have discovered them. They are claiming the Babydolls for their own, singing in unison to the chorus of "Ever After" and "Morning Ride."

They say you can't go home again. But the band that changed the musical landscape and spoke to a generation is doing just that—coming to their second home, London, but to a new crowd that is embracing them more than ever before.

Chapter Twenty-one

"Tangled Up in Blue"
—Bob Dylan

Toby has always been my hero. He's the one who has helped Dad stay sober, who showed up for my school's Christmas pageant the year my parents were in L.A. and I worried no one would be there for me and I'd be an outcast at the ripe old age of ten. He's listened to me, and he's been my friend. The night of the concert at Wembley, he even made sure I had a separate limousine so I could get back to the hotel after the show was over without having to wait for everyone.

Nick had left me phone messages apologizing for "losing his head," as he put it. He'd sent flowers. He'd slid a note under my door. But I packed for my grandparents' house and hoped to avoid seeing him. Ever since word got out that the Wolves and the Babydolls were staying in the hotel, the lobby was full of teen girls—whom management chased away—and the sidewalk was often full of stargazers. I felt like a caged hamster—everywhere we went it was pandemonium, and privacy was at a premium.

Cammie and Kai had plans for a romantic late supper after the concert at Wembley, and Toby and I decided to have dinner in his room. We ordered steak and baked potatoes and watched British television, which made us laugh.

"Toby," I said, stretching my arms upward, sleepy. It was after one in the morning. "How have you stayed sober all these years even though you're around rock-and-roll guys?"

He had on sweatpants and a T-shirt, and he looked thoughtful. "Hmm . . . good question. I guess I just remind myself every day how far I've come."

"What do you mean?"

"When I went into AA, I had this sponsor, a really cool old biker named Dave. He died about five years ago—motorcycle accident. Anyway, Dave told me to remember the worst thing that ever happened to me when I was drunk . . . the thing I was most ashamed of. And to not just remember it, but to really concentrate and think of every awful detail."

"Why would you want to do that?"

"Well, Dave said every time I was tempted to pick up a drink, I should remember that moment—remember how low I was capable of sinking—which all these years has helped me realize that no matter how much fun these guys look like they're having, the situation is just one step away from a slide down into the bottle. Sooner or later you will feel sick, ashamed, or just awful."

I nodded. "That makes sense. . . . And what about all the women? I've never seen you go for anyone backstage or anywhere."

"Liv . . . when you're younger, maybe, sex is about sex. At least it is for some guys—and girls. But when you get a little older, you realize that anonymous sex—besides being unsafe—just doesn't do much for you. Those girls who would do anything to be with the band, they're just not for me. But Lisa . . . now, she's a different story. She's smart, funny, and we have a lot in common. She's just a hell of a lot more interesting than the band bimbos. . . . Are these questions just a ploy to get insights into Nick?"

"No!"

"Come on, Liv. This is me, Toby, you're talking to."

"Well . . . maybe. I just don't like the whole scene. I like him, but not what comes along with being one of the Wolves."

"Is that really fair?"

"What do you mean?"

"Look, we all come with baggage, Liv. Some guys might be put off that your father is Paul James. That you're so independent. Or that you like to spend hours holed up in your room making compilation CDs. That you have a soundtrack to your life running in your head twenty-four/seven. That you can be exceedingly nasty before you've had a cappuccino in the morning. That . . . Well, you get the idea. We all come to the table with something. He comes with a band. Doesn't make him a bad guy, Liv. You know, the way I see it, as your friend, I think you spend your life expecting to be disappointed, so when someone hurts you just a tiny bit, you can say, 'There, I was right all along.' You like being right."

"Maybe," I whispered. Toby knew me better than I knew myself sometimes. I yawned. "Can I crash here tonight?"

"Sure thing. I've got two queens. Pick one."

I went over to one of the beds and took off my shoes. I stood on the bed and flopped backward.

"If you crack your head again . . ." He was the one to drive me to the hospital the time I hit my head doing the same thing and had to get stitches.

"I can't help it. I love doing that."

I rolled onto my side and was asleep almost instantly.

The next morning I went to my room early. Cammie wasn't there, so I left her a note telling her I would see her the next afternoon. I grabbed my backpack and walked down the hall to my parents' room. No one answered when I knocked, so I took out a sheet of notebook paper and wrote a note.

> *Dear Mom and Dad,*
>> *Left for Grandma's. See you tomorrow.*
>> *Love,*
>> *Livy*
>> *P.S.: Dad, you were awesome last night.*
> *Great show.*

A limousine waited for me to go to my grandparents' house. They lived about ten minutes from London in a big stone house that I used to think was a real castle when I was little. I wasn't that far off. It had about fourteen rooms and a couple of acres of land.

My mother found her parents disapproving. She left home and got into the club scene, and they were, as Mom put it, "a proper English family." Proper English families didn't have club kids. They had daughters who went to boarding school and married proper English gentlemen. Or they studied proper English subjects. Grandpa was a professor of music, and they expected Mom to go to a conservatory for piano. Mom had other plans.

My grandmother always wore her hair pulled up in a bun, and she had high tea each day. They dressed for supper—and I had remembered to shove a dressy top and pants into my backpack. But while they may have disapproved of my mother's path, they spoiled me rotten. I think that's in the job description for grandparents. I know it drove my mother insane that they indulged me while making it all too clear that my mother had wasted her musical talents. And let's not get started on how they felt about Paul James.

The limousine pulled up in front of the house, which Mom called "Castle de Snob." It was imposing—big gray stones and tall windows, with a heavy polished oak door easily sixteen feet high. The driver stopped, and within a second or two my grandparents were outside, holding open their arms. "Olivia!" my grandmother exclaimed. Okay, so they were the only people who could call me that and get away with it.

I climbed out of the car and rushed over and gave them each a hug and kiss. My grandfather spoke to the driver and then joined us as we went in the house.

"Where's your bag?" my grandfather asked.

"Everything's in my backpack. I travel light." I grinned.

"Olivia," Grandma said, "you are not allowed to grow a single inch taller. Are you hungry, dear?"

"Kind of."

"Wonderful. Come along. . . ." They guided me to the sun porch—a beautiful glass room off to the back of the house that overlooked rose gardens. A pot of tea was already waiting, along with scones and muffins.

The three of us sat down, and about ten minutes later their housekeeper, Mary, came to check on us, then left us alone to catch up. The wonderful thing about my grandparents is, whether it's true or not, they act as if every accomplishment is the most fantastic thing they've ever heard in their lives. Even accomplishments I have nothing to do with, such as when I was eight and lost my two front teeth.

After we caught up for an hour or so, my grandfather finally asked, "And how is your mother?"

"Good. Stressed out because of being on tour, but good."

"And your father?"

"Good."

Then silence. Finally I said, "You know, it would be nice if you came to New York for a visit and we could *all* be together."

My grandmother looked appalled. "Olivia, dear, the last time we saw your father was . . . difficult."

"Was that the year he drove his car into the pizzeria?"

"No, it was the year he pulled the Christmas tree down on top of himself and passed out."

"Oh, yeah. Hmm . . . well, you know he has been sober for a year—on his best behavior and everything."

"Oh, we'll see, darling," my grandmother said.

"Are you still planning on being a famous writer?" my grandfather asked.

I nodded. "This gig with *Rock On* will look great on my college application. I did really well on my SATs, too."

"I wish you would consider doing your third year of university here," Grandpa said.

"I keep thinking about it. Maybe I can talk Cammie into it—she's my best friend. Remember when you met her three years ago? The one with the long blond hair?"

"Oh, yes, lovely. Very pretty girl, remember, Edward?" My grandmother looked at my grandfather.

He nodded. "Do you want to take a walk on the grounds? Or do you want to get settled in your room?"

"I actually have to check my e-mail. Maybe I could go to my room for a little bit, and then the three of us can take a walk."

"Wonderful. Come upstairs, then." My grandfather rose and held out his hand, which I took. We went to the front hall and then climbed the immense staircase to the second floor. The hallway was lined with paintings of people I presumed were my relatives from way back when. It was hard to imagine that my mother came from this place—and from my grandparents. They were nothing alike.

"Your grandmother and I thought you might like to stay in your mother's old room—from when she was your age. She left home . . ." he said a little sadly, "and I suppose we kept thinking she'd come back. With so many rooms, we just never got around to changing it much."

He led me down the hall to the very last door on the right-hand side. I felt like I was stepping into a time warp.

"Holy crap! Look at all this stuff!"

"Olivia!" My grandfather's eyes widened.

"Sorry," I said sheepishly.

My mother's old room was painted a soft rose color, and the bedspread was a handmade quilt in a faded blue pattern. There was a window seat and lace curtains. And those were the only things "very proper English" about the room. The walls were covered with rock-and-roll posters: Led Zeppelin, Pink Floyd, Elton John, David Bowie, the Rolling Stones. She had a huge corkboard, and on it were pinned hundreds of pictures that she must have painstakingly cut out of magazines like *Rolling Stone* and *Creem*.

"She must have really loved music," I said.

"Yes. Darn near drove us mad. I suppose it was her way of letting us know we were behind the times. That my music—classical—wasn't interesting to her."

"You know she listens to classical music at home now. When she wants to relax."

He smiled. "See, I guess I did know a little something after all. Well, you check your e-mail. You need anything for that?"

"No. I have wireless in my laptop."

"Olivia, now I feel very, very old. Come down when you want to take our walk."

"Okay." I kissed his cheek. "I love you, Grandpa."

He flushed a little. "I love you, too."

He left, shut the door, and I turned on my computer and connected to the Internet. And got the shock of my life.

Chapter Twenty-two

"Playing Your Song"

—Hole

FR: Carl Erikson
TO: Livy James
RE: What the Hell is Going
    On?!/Attachment

Liv . . .

Please listen to the audio clip attached to this e-mail. My ace reporter in the field's been holding back!

What's on the clip? A new Wolves song that debuted ten minutes ago on a New York City radio station. It's something they played live—impromptu—during a radio interview in London. Apparently, Nick just wrote it. And if that wasn't enough . . . it made MTV's newscast.

It's a great song. And it appears to be about you! The song's called "Love, Livy."

Yup. So you wanna tell your old pal Carl what's up with you and Nick Hoffman?

By the way, I've been loving what you've sent so far. But keep me in the damn loop.

Rock On,
Carl

Chapter Twenty-three

"Boys on the Radio"
—Hole

FR: Livy James
TO: Carl Erikson
RE: Where do I begin?

Carl,
Well, at least it's a good song.
I really had no idea I was about to be the subject of a Wolves song. In Tokyo there was chemistry between Nick and me when I was interviewing him (and I really did the interview and have the tape to prove it). But I'm too busy muddling through the history of the Babydolls, to be honest. Even if I wanted to have a relationship with Nick Hoffman, I'm not too keen on repeating my parents' mistakes.
Love,
Livy

FR: Carl Erikson
TO: Livy James
RE: Sins of the father

Livy,

You want a piece of unsolicited advice? I listened to the audio clip a dozen times. There's some intense feeling in that song. So for what it's worth, everything I know about Nick Hoffman tells me he's nothing like your father. And you're too smart to be doomed to repeat your parents' mistakes. You've been following the thread of that night in Paris. What have you learned? Liv, you're your own person . . . and Nick is his own person. If I were a betting man, I'd say there's something there. Go for it—but in your own unique way.

Rock On,
Carl

P.S. All will be forgiven as far as holding back on me if you and Nick send me a picture of the two of you together to run in the magazine. Hey . . . I still have a magazine to run, you know?

Chapter Twenty-five

"With or Without You"

—U2

I finished up my e-mails and listened to the audio clip a couple of times. I felt stark naked—though I was still fully dressed. It was so strange to have a song—even a rough version of one—out there about me. I felt like now everyone knew way too much about me—but at the same time, it was exciting to think Nick had written a song just for me. Well, me and the whole damn world.

I went downstairs and took a walk with my grandparents. I held their hands and wished they would declare a truce with my mother. After our walk, I went upstairs again to shower and dress for dinner. In the bathroom, I hung the pants and top I brought, hoping the steam from the shower would get rid of some of the wrinkles.

After my shower, I opened the bathroom door to let some of the steam out but it was no use. I couldn't see in the bathroom mirror to save my life. I decided to wait a few more minutes, and sat by the window seat in my room. And then I saw it.

I spied a book tucked on a small ledge above the window seat. I reached up and pulled it down, opening the pages. It was my mother's journal, though it wasn't so much a journal as a collection of writings and lyrics and songs.

Leafing through, I could see that the words and lyrics were special. Musical notes were hand-drawn.

Excitedly, I got dressed and let my hair air-dry. I went searching for my grandfather and found him in his music room.

"Grandpa?"

"Yes, Olivia. Oh, you look beautiful."

"Thank you. Um . . . Grandpa? Have you ever seen this book before?"

He looked at it, puzzled, and then recognition crossed his face. "It was your mother's. She carried it with her everywhere—she always had it with her when she would come to visit—even when she was pregnant with you. She was always scribbling in it. I'm surprised she left it behind."

"See this song here?" I pointed to words for a song called "My Two Boys."

Grandpa nodded.

"Could you take these notes and make an actual arrangement? For piano? Or guitar?"

"I don't see why not. Why?"

"Grandpa." I sat down on the footrest by his chair. "Someone special wrote a song about me called 'Love, Livy.' And I think for some people music says things better than words. Do you know what I mean?"

"Of course I know. I've loved music for as long as I can remember—though Beethoven speaks to me more than, say, the Babydolls." He winked at me.

"Do you remember a long time ago, a night in Paris, when there was a big fight between my father and Greg Essex, Mom's old boyfriend?"

He nodded. "Before that, we had been working on repairing our relationship with your mother. We thought Greg was a terrible influence. He loved her, but he was a very, very volatile man. And then we heard about the gunfire—on the television news, of all things, and then the paper. Your grandmother nearly fainted. She had visions of you or your mother being shot one day. It nearly broke your grandmother's heart. She called your mother. Words were spoken." He shook his head.

"Well, Grandpa, I think before my mother, father, Greg, Steve, and Charlie can ever really be at peace, they have to make it right. Have some closure. That incident is always on their minds. When you're with them, and they get into a disagreement, it's the first thing anyone says, the first thing anyone thinks of. Will someone pull a gun? Will it get out of hand?"

"Terrible . . ."

"It is terrible. But this song in this jounral is really beautiful. She talks about both Greg and my father and how they were two parts of her soul. How she was so torn, but that she knew they would be better off if she chose one and let the other go free. She talks about the good qualities in both, and how her heart hurt from the decision. I think if I can get this song into the hands of each of the Babydolls, and let them surprise her with it, then maybe things will be better. Greg and my father will figure out they don't need to be jealous of each other. She loved each of them for different reasons. Will you help me?"

He took the notebook and held it closer to him, reading it, studying it. Then he smiled. "You realize we'll have to

157

stay up late—it will be downright wild around here. Rock and roll on my piano!" He started laughing . . . and I laughed along with him.

"It will be good for you and Mom and Grandma, too. Thank you." I threw my arms around his neck and kissed him, knocking his glasses off his head.

"Olivia . . . you are a breath of fresh air around here."

Chapter Twenty-six

"Behind Blue Eyes"
—The Who

My grandfather and I shut ourselves in his music room after dinner. My grandmother seemed excited by the project. She bustled in and out bringing pots of tea, chocolates, biscuits, cookies, cheese, and fruit. It certainly beat Cammie's and my typical all-nighter food.

Grandpa laid sheet music out on top of his shiny black baby grand piano. He would play chords and then scribble, then erase, play new chords, scribble more. As he wrote out the music, he said to me, "Your mother's talent is extraordinary, Livy. I can't believe she wrote this. It's very sophisticated."

He worked on the chorus, and I helped adjust a few words in the lyrics so that it flowed more smoothly. My grandfather and I were sharing in this experience, and I felt closer to my mother at the same time. The whole notebook was filled with amazing words and poetry. It reminded me that my mother was my age once. She was a club kid; she lived through music.

At midnight, my grandmother poked her head in again. "Is it done?"

"Just about." My grandfather made a few more scribbles. "Listen."

He began playing the song, as he had arranged it, on the

piano. He didn't sing the words, but I heard them in my mind: *My two boys, who taught me heartache, soul ache, love take . . . me away from the pain of choosing, my two boys, my two boys.*

The music, on the piano, was soulful. It reminded me of Fiona Apple, Dido, or Natalie Merchant. When my grandfather was finished playing, Grandma and I applauded.

Grandma's eyes were moist. "So lovely. My girl is so talented."

"I have an idea."

Grandpa turned toward me on the piano bench. "What, dear?"

"Come to Wembley. Tomorrow night. Say you'll come."

"We couldn't possibly."

"No, listen . . . Toby is our bodyguard and driver. He can arrange it so you walk right into VIP seating. You can surprise her. I'll talk them all into playing this song. Then, when it plays, we'll announce that you did the arrangement. Oh, please, Grandpa? Please, please, please, please? Remember when I used to ask for a horse for Christmas? I'll never ask for a horse again, I swear it."

They both laughed. Grandma said, "Us? At a rock concert? Olivia, there must be something in the tea. I'll ask Mary . . . she must have spiked it with something, child. It will be too loud, too crowded."

"Don't be scared. Do you trust me?"

They both looked solemnly at me. "Of course we do," my grandfather said.

"Then leave this to me. Okay?"

They didn't say anything for a minute or two.

Finally Grandpa said, "We do love her, so if you think that—"

"Oh! I just know this will work!" I leaped toward him and gave him a hug, then her. Then I took the music and clutched it to my chest. "Good night. I've got to go upstairs and make some phone calls."

"At this hour?" my grandmother said.

"Grandma, rock and roll never sleeps!"

Chapter Twenty-seven

"Hard Charger"
—Porno for Pyros

I stayed up until three o'clock in the morning. Toby was my first call, and he thought my plan was crazy, yet had a touch of genius. He was in. He would figure out transportation, seating, and bodyguards and escorts for my grandparents. He would also arrange to get them some earplugs.

I called my father next, on his cell phone, so there'd be no chance my mother would answer. I told him my idea, and he sneaked into the bathroom so he could talk without Mom overhearing. He thought the idea was absurd—but had elements of brilliance.

Charlie was easy. He was sober, he wanted closure, and he had taken my suggestion the night of our walk through Tokyo and called Serena, who had started crying on the phone that she missed him. It looked like they had a chance of getting back together, so that meant that he owed me one.

Steve Zane didn't answer the phone until two thirty in the morning, when he got in from the pubs. I told him the whole story, and he shocked me by saying yes. I didn't even have to talk him into it!

That left Greg Essex. And the only way I could even hope to get him to say yes was to speak to him alone. At three o'clock I finally shut my eyes, but visions of Nick Hoffman filled my mind. I fantasized about kissing him until I thought my head would explode. Then I dozed off until Grandma came in at seven to wake me up. I had asked her to wake me early so I could get back to the hotel as soon as possible. She opened the door and came in with a pot of tea.

"Here you go, Olivia, dear."

"Coffee. Please. I'm begging you as your only grand-child."

"But tea is so much better, Olivia. And you need your strength today."

"Please, Grandma?"

"Oh, all right. I'll have Mary bring you up a cup."

"A pot."

"What, dear?"

"A pot. A pot of coffee."

She chuckled and said, "Yes, dear."

I rolled out of bed. Forget makeup. Time was of the essence. Fifteen minutes later, after I'd washed my face with ice-cold water, pinched my cheeks, brushed my teeth, and run a brush through my hair, Mary came in with cof-fee, which I chugged and burned my tongue. It was terrible. The English really *can't* make a good pot of coffee. I raced downstairs. Grandpa said the limo had arrived. Thank God for Toby.

I kissed my grandparents good-bye and told them Toby would be sending them a driver and two escorts for the concert.

"Wear sneakers."

"We don't own sneakers, dear," Grandma said.

"Sensible shoes?"

"That we have," she answered.

"Good. See you later."

I left the house and climbed in the car. I asked the driver to take me to a copy store. I needed to make four copies of the music, which I did. Then we raced on to London and the hotel.

The elevator didn't go fast enough. I was so antsy for this to work out. I got off at my floor and raced to my room. I let myself in *very* quietly, in case Cam and Kai were there. She was sitting on her bed cross-legged.

"Toby told me you were coming home early. Well, do I look different?"

"No, why?"

"Operation V. Mission accomplished."

I laughed. "I don't know whether to congratulate you, ask for all the gory details, or what?"

"Oh, Liv. It was really beautiful. I'm so glad it was Kai. He had flowers and champagne, and music. He was so sweet. It was awesome."

"I'm really happy for you."

"I know. So do I look different?"

I took a step backward and eyed her up and down. "No. But you are *glowing.*"

"Oh, shut up! And what is this top-secret mission you're on?"

I sat down on her bed and told her, showing her the music.

"Take this one to Charlie, and this one to my dad. If my

mom answers the door, just tell her you were wondering what time I'm coming home . . . then leave. My dad will come find you—say he's going out for cigarettes or something."

"What about Steve Zane?"

"I don't trust you with him yet."

"Don't be silly. I think I'm in love. I'm not interested in the bad boy anymore."

"All right, this one's for Steve."

I handed her one of the copies of music. "I have to go see Greg."

"I wouldn't wish that on anyone. You should have seen him last night. Obliterated."

"Great," I said unenthusiastically. "This should be a piece of cake."

I took the sheet music and left our room for Greg's. I knocked on the door.

No answer.

I knocked louder.

No answer.

I knocked a *lot* louder. I heard him hurl a lamp at the door. At least I think it was a lamp. It crashed.

"Greg! It's Livy."

"Fuck, piss, shit, fuck! Get lost!"

"Please let me in."

I waited a few minutes, knocking every now and then, and finally I heard him fumbling with the door.

"What in God's heaven do you want at this hour?"

"I have to talk to you. It's really, really important."

"Jeez . . . fine. Make it quick."

I walked in, my hands shaking as I clutched the music.

"Greg . . ." I turned to face him—and noticed he was naked. I kept my eyes focused on his face, and continued. "Um . . . okay . . . here it is. My mother loved you."

"And left me. We all know that."

"No, she loved you even as she was leaving, even after she moved in with my father. She loved you and she loved him. She wrote a song about you. About both of you."

He stared at me, and I didn't know if he was still drunk or just mad at me for waking him up.

"It's called 'My Two Boys,' and Greg, it's beautiful. It explains everything she was thinking. And it makes so much sense in music—more sense than in life."

He gave a half laugh. "Ain't that the truth about almost everything?"

"Just look at it." I thrust the music at him. "Everyone else in the band is up for playing this tonight. For her. For the band, for the friendships you once had. My grandfather and I stayed up all night arranging it. We want to surprise her. Please say you'll do it."

He read the music and the lyrics, and he turned his back to me. He walked away, into his bathroom, and came back with a robe on.

"Well?"

He looked at me, and tears were streaming down his face. "I can't talk."

He walked over to the minibar and took out a beer—at eight o'clock in the morning. Not my breakfast beverage of choice, but I hoped that was a sign he was thinking about it. Greg seemed to think better when he drank beer.

166

He rubbed his face and then went to his guitar case and took it out. He had an acoustic guitar, a twelve-string acoustic, and four Fender electric guitars. He sat down on his bed, laid the sheet music next to him, and started playing softly, quietly, humming, then eventually singing some of the lyrics. I was so used to him and my dad sort of growling their songs, so hearing him sing softly was really beautiful. My mom was right—he had a lovely voice.

"Thank you, Liv," he finally said.

"For what?"

"This." He touched the sheet of music. "I know that I'm not the settling-down type, and that maybe everything happened for the best, but this makes me feel better about it—that I meant something to her."

"So you'll play it tonight?"

"Yeah. We'll rehearse a bit this afternoon, then."

"Oh, thank you, Greg," I ran to him and kissed him.

He gave me a hug and then I turned and left. Still so much to do before the concert.

Chapter Twenty-eight

I felt like I had one last thing to do before going to my room, crashing, and then getting ready for the concert—to make up with Nick.

I thought of how I felt when I heard certain songs. Like I had flopped straight back on my bed, like I was falling, like I was floating, like I was lost in a moment. Certain songs made me want to listen to them over and over and over again. I could feel them in my gut. I felt that way when I heard "Candy's Room" by Bruce Springsteen, or "Black Hole Sun," or . . . when I heard the Cult sometimes. I could get lost in Annie Lennox's voice. And there were moments, in the pit of my stomach, when I really gave myself over to a song. When I had headphones on and shut my eyes, and stopped being me and became song, word, notes. It was a leap of faith, music. You had to let go of the world if you ever really wanted to get lost in it. If you ever really wanted to *know*, really know what music is.

I decided love was the same thing. You were scared, sure. You could fall backward and land on softness, or fall backward and need ten stitches. It could go either way.

To get the most out of love, you just had to close your eyes and jump.

So I decided to do that.

I got off on the floor the Wolves were staying on and walked to Nick's room. I knocked on the door.

"Just a minute . . ." Nick's voice came from the other side.

He had written "Love, Livy" for me. My heart pounded.

He opened the door, stared for a minute, and grabbed me, pulling me to him and kissing me hard on the mouth.

"Oh, God, you are a sight for sore eyes."

I kissed him back, feeling like I was floating. Then we stopped for a minute and I looked past him into his room— and was stunned. There sat a girl. Not just any girl, really, but a beautiful girl.

He looked at me. "Oh, wait, Liv . . . I can explain this."

"Don't bother. I don't know what I was thinking."

The girl stood up. "Wait!" she said, looking upset, but I couldn't take it. I turned and ran down the hall, but he followed, grabbing my wrist and spinning me around.

"She's a backup singer. Don't you recognize her from the song 'Sweet Murder'?"

"No, I don't."

"Well, you've seen her before. Onstage."

I tried to think back to his concerts. I was usually so focused on him that I could barely remember anyone else at all.

"Livy . . . I swear to you nothing's going on. At some point you have to trust me. She came to rehearse a song we screwed up the other night—no one else noticed, but I did. And she's been listening to me fookin' blather on about you."

He pulled me to him again. Before I felt like I was free-falling; now I just felt like I was crashing.

"Are you going to the concert tonight?"

I nodded.

"I'll see you afterward. We can talk. Okay? Promise me you won't run away from me."

I didn't say anything.

"Promise me, Livy."

Reluctantly, I said, "I promise."

"I was a jerk that night, the night I'd been drinking. And you were right to tell me to shove off. You're too special for that, Liv. But I won't make that mistake again. You're going to have to have faith."

I nodded and turned and walked away. Would I ever be able to trust a rocker?

I didn't know, and part of me was too afraid to find out.

Chapter Twenty-nine

"Everybody's Gonna Be Happy"
—The Kinks

The bus to Wembley was different from any other tour bus I had been on. It looked the same as all of them. Same stocked bar, cushy seats, flat-screen televisions, and piped-in music. But the energy was different.

All four Babydolls were sober. That was a first. And they were acting differently toward one another. No one was bickering or picking a fight. And when Dad and Charlie and Toby held hands and said the Serenity Prayer, Steve and Greg joined in.

My mom seemed oblivious to it all, which was good. But everyone kept looking at her expectantly. It was hard to keep the secret.

We arrived at the stadium and settled into the backstage area. When it was time for the Wolves to go on, Toby asked me, my mom, and Cam to come with him backstage.

"Come on; let's all watch them together."

My mother shrugged and came along. I knew Toby was doing this to be absolutely certain she didn't run into my grandparents in the VIP section.

We settled into our seats, and Nick and the band were introduced. He grabbed the microphone and said, his voice reverberating throughout the stadium, "This is our new song, not on any CD yet, still working out the kinks, but it goes out to my girl."

They sang "Love, Livy," and Cammie kept elbowing me. "I want a song for me one day," she said.

I laughed, and listened. At some point in the music I did a free fall. I fell backward into the song and disappeared.

Nick told me the goal of Buddhism was loss of self—to become so at peace that the self's selfish goals and aims were gone and the person was in total harmony with the world. My self was gone into the music, lost in a world that was Nick and words and notes.

During two songs I spied the backup singer. She was one of two girls who sang on a couple of songs, and I felt mildly better. When their set was over, the crowd gave them thunderous applause that made the whole stadium feel like it was shaking.

After a very brief break, the Babydolls were introduced. They opened with "The Sky Is Falling," and then moved on to "Killing Angel." My father came to the front of the stage and looked right at the VIP section, then over to the wings of the stage, where we were. He motioned for the crowd to settle down, which they did, and I marveled at the godlike power of his magnetism.

"We have a very, very special song for you tonight. This is a first—the Babydolls have never performed this. In fact, no one has."

The crowd cheered, and he motioned again for them to be quiet.

"This was written a while ago by my beautiful wife,

Anna. The arrangement was done by her father, Professor Edward Scott of Oxford. It's called 'My Two Boys,' and we hope you think it's as brilliant as we do."

While my father was talking, Greg had put down his Fender and had taken up his acoustic guitar. Without screaming or wailing, they began the soft, elegant strains my mother had written sixteen or seventeen years before.

One my lover
One my friend
My two boys
My two boys
Can't live without either
Lover, lover, friend,
My two boys

Cammie and I looked at my mother. She was crying, but they looked like happy tears. Toby gave me the thumbs-up sign.

When the Babydolls were finished, the crowd went insane. But that wasn't the most amazing thing. My father walked over to Greg and grabbed him in the fiercest bear hug I'd ever seen. The two men clutched each other on the stage; then Steve came over, and Charlie left his drum set and shared in the hug that went on as long as the crowd whistled and screamed.

They made rock history. They became a band of brothers again.

My mother turned to me. "You?"

I nodded, and she grabbed me tightly.

The show went on from there. It was amazing because without all the hatred between them, the Babydolls played better than ever.

After the concert Toby escorted us to the dressing room area. My father was already hugging my grandparents. My mother froze when she saw them; then she went running over to her father like a little girl and threw her arms around his neck. Cammie and I walked over to them.

"I'm so sorry." My mother was sobbing into her father's neck.

"No, we are. It's been too long, darling."

My mother hugged Grandma, and then my father hugged them all again and gave my mother a huge, long kiss that ordinarily would have made me cringe, but, well, it was the moment.

Greg stood off to the side, and then my mother ran to him and kissed his cheek and hugged him. They didn't say anything to each other, but I think I saw them speak with their eyes. They told each other all was forgiven.

My mother came over to me again, with my father. "Liv, I'm not sure how you pulled this off, but . . ."

I shrugged.

My father kissed me, then my mom. She held me to her, and then she whispered something ever so softly in my ear: "If you love him, don't be afraid. . . ."

I stepped back from her and nodded.

Even George the Vampire looked happy. Ecstatic, really. "That single will make us millions."

That was George for you.

Kai and Nick came and found us all. Nick shook my father's hand and then each band member's in turn. "Phenomenal show." He complimented my mother's song and shook hands with my grandfather.

Cammie and I left with them. "Mind if we don't go pub crawling tonight?" Nick whispered in my ear as we climbed into the limousine.

"Not at all," I said, grinning.

So it was very high school, the two couples making out in the backseat. Kind of like prom night.

We got back to our hotel, and as usual, a bunch of autograph hounds were screaming when we got out of the car. But I didn't mind them so much. Maybe I finally accepted that he was mine.

Cam and Kai went to Kai's room, and Nick and I went to his room. He had champagne chilling and popped the cork.

"I don't ever want to fight again."

"Me, either," I whispered.

"Do you like your song?"

I nodded.

"What you did for the Babydolls was beautiful."

"Thanks."

"You gave them closure. You gave them each other again."

"I did it for me, as much as for them. For my parents."

He came close, and I shivered. He pulled me to him and kissed me, gently at first, then harder. They were definitely grown-up kisses.

"I'm afraid," I said.

"Of me?"

I nodded. I never wanted to be like my mother. But I started to realize you could rewrite the music any way you wanted.

"I'm falling for you, Liv."

"I think I fell in Tokyo."

"Wait one minute." He pulled away from me and went to the door and put the DO NOT DISTURB sign on the knob. Then he came back and kissed me on my neck.

"I like falling with you."

So we went to the bed and fell.

Chapter Thirty

TO: Carl Erikson
FR: Livy James
RE: Postcard from L.A./attachment

Hi, Carl.

Well, you got my exclusive interview with my mother, the hottest new songwriter on the scene. And attached is a picture of Nick and me in L.A. You can run it in your gossip section.

Things have really changed. Greg is off all drugs, and even Steve has slowed down some. Greg and my dad seemed to pick up where they left off. And my mother is suddenly like den mother to the band again. Both bands. She really loves the Wolves.

The tour wraps up in two weeks, and it's been the most amazing summer of my life. I fell in love, I forgave my parents, I learned a lot about music, and about not being afraid of los-ing control. It's okay to get your heart broken, as long as it's in the name of love. But I think you knew that. I think when you sent me on this odyssey to write the story of the Babydolls, you knew a lot of what I would find.

When the tour is over, it's back to school for Cam and me—only we will officially have the hottest boyfriends in school. Nick has an apartment in New York. He'll spend time there. Kai has a place in L.A., but he'll fly in and out.

So . . . here it is. The story of the Babydolls. Thanks, Carl, for everything.

The Babydolls were forever altered by that night in Paris. Everyone—from the media to the fans to the deejays pontificating on rock radio—thought they knew the whole story. But one thing this tour taught everyone is that there's no such thing as the whole story.

Every person who was there that night in Paris has a different truth about what happened. The hardest thing to learn in life is that there may be no truth—not really. Not in black and white. The truth changes for each person who tells it.

At first, as the daughter of Paul James, that bothered me. But then I realized that it made perfect sense. Music changes for each person who hears it. I hear a song and lose myself in it—the next person may feel nothing. You like rap; I like rock. You like—God help us all—pop. I like the blues. Whatever it is that speaks to you, it's your truth. Your music.

So that night in Paris was about different things for different people: loss, pain, betrayal, love, passion, friendship, despair, hope, belief in another, loss of faith in another. I realized I could never write what really happened, because what really happened depends on which player you're referring to.

This summer tour changed me. Not only did I learn that truth is relative, I learned that sometimes you just have to get lost in love and music. It's part of youth. It's part of what you owe yourself. You have to go to the edge of the rock-and-roll abyss and jump in with both feet. It's like leaping off the stage into a mosh pit. You just have to take a leap of faith. You just have to Rock On.

Liza Conrad lives in south Florida. She grew up listening to Led Zeppelin, Bruce Springsteen, the Clash, and later loved John Hiatt, Elvis Costello, Pearl Jam, and a list too long to even mention. Her favorite rock song of all time is "Sympathy for the Devil" by the Rolling Stones—or maybe "Cocaine" by Eric Clapton. Or "The Rising" by Bruce Springsteen. On second thought, it's way too hard to think of only one. When she was a teen she pierced her own ear five times one day when she was bored, and she loved to go to concerts. Now, in her free time, when she's not writing or listening to music, she enjoys playing with her dog, going to the beach, and being with her family and friends. She is at work on her next novel, as well as a screenplay, and she can be reached at her Web site at www.lizaconrad.com.

Don't you just love
cool new novels like

ROCK MY WORLD

A Novel of Thongs, Spandex,
and Love in G Minor?

Now here's a preview of two books
just like it that rock!

Turn the page to sample

Trish Cook's

SO LYRICAL

(on sale now)

and

Emily Franklin's

THE PRINCIPLES OF LOVE

(on sale July 2005)

books

COMING THIS SUMMER
A TOTALLY FRESH LINE OF BOOKS

<u>June 2005</u>
SO LYRICAL
by Trish Cook
0-451-21508-7

<u>July 2005</u>
THE PRINCIPLES OF LOVE
by Emily Franklin
0-451-21517-6

CONFESSIONS OF AN ALMOST-MOVIE STAR
by Mary Kennedy
0-425-20467-7

<u>August 2005</u>
ROCK MY WORLD
by Lisa Conrad
0-451-21523-0

JENNIFER SCALES AND THE ANCIENT FURNACE
by MaryJanice Davidson
and Anthony Alongi
0-425-20598-3

Available in paperback from Berkley and New American Library

www.penguin.com

So Lyrical

by Trish Cook

"Trace!"

I stuck my head out of my locker and scanned the between-class mosh pit. A blur of faces surfed by, none of which seemed to belong to anyone in desperate need of me. Taking a deep breath, I went back to my excavation. I finally found what I was looking for underneath a week-old lunch bag.

"Gotcha," I muttered, unearthing my trig book. Pens, crumpled papers, and unwashed gym clothes all came flying out after it. I tossed the scrambled mess back inside, slamming the door and throwing myself against it for good measure. I could totally understand the escape attempt. It reeked like tuna and old sweat in there.

"Trace!"

There was that voice again, only louder and more pissed off this time. I scoped the halls until I finally spotted the screamer—otherwise known as my best friend, Sabrina Maldonati. Her body-hugging skirt and sky-high heels made navigating the polished marble floors of Northshore Regional High School a tough proposition. Think beached mermaid and you'll get the picture.

If I could only fast-forward her, I thought, glancing at my watch and hoping I wasn't going to be late for class.

Brina made her grand entrance a moment later clutching a piece of paper to her more-than-ample chest.

"Stop bitching and start reading," she said. "Because this is the most unbelievable thing ever."

I faked a big yawn. "Can't Harvard just take no for an answer?" The more over-the-top she gets, the more I like to yank her chain.

"Not funny."

"Your mom wrote a note so you don't have to face the fat calipers in gym today?"

Brina shook her head so hard I thought brains would come flying out her ears in wrinkly pieces. "Wrong again. And anyway, you know how I feel about the *F* word."

"What, fu—"

"Uh, uh, uh. You quit swearing, remember?" Brina said, interrupting me just in the nick of time. "And the word I was referring to is 'fat.' Last night, my mom offered to get me liposuction for my eighteenth birthday."

"You're so full of—"

"Trace, you're gonna have to try a lot harder if you're serious about cleaning up your language."

"I was about to say 'malarkey.' "

"One of us is lying," said Brina. "Here's a hint. It's not me."

She was right. I wouldn't be caught dead saying anything remotely like, "You're so full of malarkey." That meant the lipo story must be true. Brina's mom, being the anorexic lunatic that she is, probably decided fat-sucking cash was the most thoughtful, generous gift in the history of mankind.

The reality is this: Brina has an eye-popping, curvaceous bod. But instead of realizing that boobs and a butt are normal—even desirable—parts of a woman's figure, all Mrs. Maldonati can see is rolls, rolls and more rolls. In her wildest dreams, Brina suddenly turns into whichever Olsen twin is the dangerously skinny one. "Don't hold your breath" and "not in this lifetime" are two choice phrases that come to mind, but Mrs. Maldonati refuses to give up hope just yet.

"So if it isn't from Harvard and it's not a reprieve from the claw, what *is* the most unbelievable thing ever?" I asked.

"An anonymous note. Signed by 'slp.' I don't know whether to be flattered or call the cops."

So maybe this really *was* something worth getting excited about. "Hand it over," I told her.

Brina passed the note my way and breathed down my neck. I could almost hear her lips moving behind me as I read.

> Brina,
> I like to watch you from afar
> Always know just where you are
> But not where this might lead
> Maybe you could walk with me
> slp

A lone bead of sweat trickled down my back. Was I jealous? Hell, yeah. Here was some pretty awesome poetry, sweet without being sickening, warm without losing its cool. And once again, I was relegated to the lumpy, frumpy sidekick role—Quasimodo next to Brina's Esmeralda.

"Honestly? It's amazing," I admitted.

"That's what I thought," she said, folding the paper carefully and zipping it into a little compartment in the front of her notebook. I hated how she could be so neat. I also hated that her boobs were so big, and that mine were so nonexistent.

"So what are you going to do about it?" I asked her.

"Do? Nothing." We took a couple more steps before she said, "Why? What would you do?"

"I'd go walk with him."

Brina rolled her eyes.

"I'm serious," I told her.

"Oh, please. Why would I want to stroll around with some loser who's too scared to ask me out?" Brina said, doing a quick one-eighty and dismissing slp as yesterday's news. "Let's just forget about it."

I cleared my throat as a new thought came to me. This would be a kick if it actually turned out to be true. "Maybe slp is a she," I suggested. Brina may have had all the guys in school drooling after her, but up until now she hadn't done a thing for the chicks. "Your Sss-sss-secret Le-le-lesbian Puh-puh-pal." I emphasized the letters so she'd catch my drift.

Brina didn't even stop to consider my theory. "Sorry, Trace. It's just not my thing. If my pal's a gal, we're gonna have to stay friends."

I took one last crack at it. "Have you ever considered it might just be Some Lovesick Puppy?"

"Shut up, Trace, and walk. We've gotta get to trig."

Brina and I slipped into our seats as the final bell was ringing. I kept rereading the note in my mind, trying to figure
out who slp might really be. And why he—like every other
guy I knew—found Brina so intriguing, and me so not.

Stanley Larsen Pratt?

Spencer Louis Perog?

Shawn Leonard Pearsall?

All great guesses. If any these names belonged to anyone we knew, that is. And they didn't.

Minutes passed before I, being the incredibly brilliant
person I am, solved the slp mystery. There he was—Sam
Parish, a cute enough guy if you could overlook his con-
stant sniffling—slumped down in his seat with his feet
stuffed under Brina's chair.

I got all excited and passed her a note.

> Brina:
> Don't look now, but I think slp's behind you. If his middle
> name is Lester or Langley or Lancelot or Lars, it's him.
> Identity crisis over.
> Trace
> P.S. Maybe it's not an allergy or drug problem like we
> thought. He could just be trying to inhale your
> pheromones, or whatever they're called.

She read it and scribbled back.

> Trace:
> Good detective work. Let's see if he passes the test.
> slp's girlfriend

While the rest of the class was trying to calculate the Pythagorean cosine tangent of the something or other, Brina casually leaned back and whispered, "What's your middle name, hon?"

Sam pointed to his chest—honestly, he looked a little scared—and mouthed, "Me?" Then he just sat there staring at Brina with his mouth hanging open.

She finally patted his arm and whispered, "That's OK. You can tell me later." Brina turned her attention back to the nasty problem at hand, and Sam scrunched down even farther in his seat. He looked like he wanted the floor to swallow him up because he'd just ruined his one big chance with Brina. Or who knows? Maybe he was just trying to hide a huge boner.

Scratch, scratch. Fold, fold. Brina chucked the note back to me.

> Trace:
> Don't think it's him. Far too shy to have the balls to send me an anonymous love note. He might write one, but I think that's about as far as it would go.
> B

Maybe, maybe not, I thought. He could also be embarrassed at being outed so quickly by gifted me. Scribble, scribble, toss, toss.

> B:
> Let's keep him on the list for now. I'll put it right next to the one about my dad on my locker door.
> T

The other list was necessary because, unless his name really was Mike Graphone like it says on my birth certificate, I don't know a thing about my father. And as cool as my mother is in other respects—especially compared to my friends' parents—she's unbelievably uptight and close-mouthed about everything related to Daddy dearest. The only suspects I've been able to pinpoint so far are total shots in the dark: the guys I see hugging my mom in pictures hung around the rock-and-roll shrine otherwise known as my house.

Scritchy-scratchy. Flitter-flutter. Plip-plop. Mr. Flagstaff's eyes darted around the room until they came to rest on the note Brina had just thrown my way. It was just lying there on my desk looking guilty.

"Care to try your hand at the board, Tracey?" he asked.

"Sure thing, Mr. Flagstaff," I said in as cheerful a voice as I could muster. Maybe a little enthusiasm would make him forget I hadn't been paying attention for the past half an hour. Since day one, if I'm being totally honest.

But nothing could have saved me. I had no clue how to even start the problem, no less solve it. I stumbled and bumbled with the chalk, creating a powdery mess that made no sense. Not nearly soon enough, the Staffman put me out of my misery.

"Perhaps some extra homework problems will help you catch up to the rest of the class, Miss Tillingham. Your notes tonight will have a lot less to do with your social life and a lot more to do with trigonometry now, won't they?"

I gave him my best conciliatory look and saw a night of terminal boredom and frustration in my future. Once again,

Brina had been my partner in crime and I was the only one captured.

Why wasn't I the least bit surprised? Because it happened all the time. Farty old Mr. Flagstaff probably had a crush on her, like every other man on earth. Having the world's most desirable girl as my best friend was really beginning to suck the big wazoo, no matter how much I liked her.

I went directly to my room after school and changed into my workout clothes. I thought maybe a long, hard run might help me focus on the fact that I was not, contrary to what my mind would have me believing today, the world's biggest loser. Me, my Brooks sneakers, and my beloved green iPod mini were all halfway out the door before my mom stopped me dead in my tracks.

"Hey, Bebe," I said, grabbing a Balance bar and shoving it down my throat. Though my mom's real name is Belinda, I've called her Bebe since I could string a few sounds together. She says that at the time, "Mommy" was just too weird—after all, she was still teenager herself—and the whole shebang proved to be too big of a mouthful for one-year-old me.

"So Brina got a secret love note today, huh?" Bebe asked.

I swallowed fast. "How'd you find that out?"

"She called and when I asked how her day was, she said, 'Great! I got a secret love note today.' "

"Subtle."

"So what did it say, anyway?"

"Something about watching her from afar and not knowing where things will lead," I said. "Oh, and that maybe Brina should walk *with* him."

Bebe ran her fingers through her hair, looking a little puzzled.

"What?"

"Nothing," she said. "It just sounds familiar and I can't figure out why."

"Right. Well, wouldn't you know it, even the sensitive, poetic types are falling for Brina now."

"Pisses you off, huh?" Bebe put her arm around me and squeezed my shoulder.

"Yup," I said. "I guess should be happy for her?" I didn't mean for it to, but it came out as a question.

"Nahhhh. It would piss me off, too." It's almost eerie how Bebe always understands exactly how I'm feeling. The fact that we've never been through that "I hate you" phase most mothers and daughters hit at some point during high school makes me extremely lucky—I know. But when your mom: (*a*) is younger than everyone else's parents by at least ten years, (*b*) was a groupie back in the eighties (regardless of whether the overwhelming majority of bands she worshipped were kinda, sorta lame even then and definitely ancient history now), and (*c*) has morphed herself into a successful author of Harlequin-ish romances starring fictional musicians, it's easy to see how we'd relate better than most.

Bebe mercifully dropped the subject of me being caught hunching along alongside Brina yet again. "You going for a long one today?"

I gulped down some prerun water. "Eight miles. Why, you need me?"

"My agent always thinks going to a show will inspire my next book, so he bribed me with these," Bebe said, waving a couple of familiar-looking rectangles at me. "Got tenth-row tix to see the luscious Hall and Oates tonight."

"Who's luscious?" I asked her. "Hall or Oates?" I can never keep them straight.

"I don't play favorites," Bebe said, licking her lips, just in case I didn't realize she thinks they are fine, so divine. Believe me, I got it well before the spit dried.

"Can't go, Bebe," I said, thankful for my math punishment now. I mean, yikes. No one's heard from those guys in twenty years. "Flagstaff caught me passing notes in trig class and I ended up with extra homework. Brina got off the hook, of course."

"Don't sweat it. Your teacher was probably blinded by her boobs." Bebe put down the tickets and picked up the phone. "I'll just call Trixie to come with me," she said, hitting the speed dial. Trixie is Bebe's one and only Winnetka friend.

Bebe ended up here—in the world's most conservative suburb—once it became apparent that she had picked up more than just waitressing experience at the shore during her eighteenth summer. Once she started showing, Bebe got shipped off to Great-aunt Betty's house in Winnetka under the guise that it would do her some good to get out of New Jersey for a while. The truth is, it made for a lot less explaining. Never mind the fact that Bebe's parents—my grandma and grandpa Tillingham—are so cute yet so clueless, they're probably still wondering why Bebe hasn't been nominated for sainthood, what with her having had an immaculate conception and all.

To this day, Bebe says living in Winnetka is her sacrifice to me; she wanted me to have as normal an upbringing as possible, given the circumstances. And I can't imagine a better place for a kid to grow up, or a more unsuitable one for Bebe. I mean, she just doesn't blend. Instead of wearing tennis whites and listening to NPR in a luxury SUV, Bebe has holey-kneed jeans and cruises around in beat-up Beetle cranking Quiet Riot or some other band that horrifies both me and the Winnetka ladies, though for different reasons. I'm embarrassed; they're disturbed by the noise.

"Sure, Trace would love to watch the kids until John gets home from his meeting," Bebe was saying into the phone a minute later, winking at me. And I was pretty grateful for the job—even if she didn't have the courtesy to ask me first—because I might as well make some money while slaving over my math punishment.

The slp note, trig torture, and my nonexistent dad kept rolling around in my mind when I first started my run. But after a mile or two I went into the brain-dead zone, happily listening to my latest and greatest playlist and singing along whenever the spirit moved me.

My mind made it back to the land of the living when I noticed an extremely cute guy jogging alongside of me. OK, he wasn't just jogging: he was laughing. At me. I stopped singing and started scowling. What a reality slap—there was no soundproof bubble surrounding me when I had headphones on like I'd always imagined.

I shot the guy my best pissed-off Jersey Girl look—honed during our annual two-week summer vacation at Long Beach Island with my sweet 'n' ditzy grandparents—and kept running. He didn't seem the least bit intimidated and stayed in stride with me.

"You like Jimmy Eat World a lot, huh?"

I ignored him, even though I was impressed. They're not the world's most well-known band—not yet, at least.

"Know how I guessed?" he asked, belting out their song "The Sweetness" in way too good of a voice. Even all the woah-oh-ohhh-ohhh-ohs sounded right. And to think, his ears were the recipients of my most recent off-key, a cappella solo. Even worse, after hearing him sing the right ones, I was pretty sure there was a place waiting for me in the Misheard-Lyrics Hall of Fame.

"See?" he said, grinning at me.

"Sorry I offended your virgin ears, Mr. Rock Star." All the good comebacks would no doubt torture me tonight while I was tossing and turning in bed, trying to sleep.

"Not offended," he said, flashing a killer smile. "Not a virgin, either."

Hard as I tried to stay mad, I ended up laughing instead. He took it as encouragement.

"I'm Zander O'Brien," he said, sticking out his hand.

I stared at his long, tapered fingers, not sure what to do with them. After all, we were still moving at a nine-minute-mile pace. I just couldn't imagine the mechanics of the whole thing working out.

Zander gave up on the doomed handshake thing, using that arm to pump again. "How long you running for?" he asked, panting.

By now, the adrenaline shooting through me had picked my pace up to sprint. "Almost done. I'm on my last mile."

Zander seemed like he was about ready to pass out. "Want to hit . . . Starbucks . . . so we can talk . . . without me . . . gasping . . . for . . . breath?"

"Sounds great, but I gotta get home. I have to babysit tonight so my mom can go to the Hall and Oates show."

Zander stopped short. "You do?"

I stopped, too. "Yup."

"I don't think my mother has ever even been to a concert. And the only tunes she listens to are by guys who died a million years ago. You know, like Elvis and the Beatles."

"Not all of the Beatles are dead," I had to point out. "There are Elvis sightings all the time. And Hall and Oates haven't had a hit since the eighties."

"Whatever," Zander said. "At least you don't have to leave the house whenever your mom puts her music on."

If he only knew. "I wouldn't go that far," I told him. "But I will admit, my mom is pretty unique. And we're both really into music."

That's a gigantic understatement. My mom spends her days writing, and cranking out tunes that everyone else— with the exception of those retro shows—forgot decades ago. A dilapidated jukebox in the corner of our basement plays Bebe's prehistoric 45s. The portable turntable left over from her childhood spins the stacks and stacks of albums she spent her entire allowance on growing up. And her boom box, circa 1989, plays the songs contained on the seventeen thousand little cassettes that keep threatening to take over the attic someday.

Thankfully, a brand-new, state-of-the-art home entertainment system in the living room takes care of our continuously growing mountain of CDs. Because I want to save my music from any premature aging, I've separated the CDs into two piles: hers and mine. And it's easy to tell whose is whose. Bebe owns the ones only Oldies 101.5 would play; my bands rock MTV2.

To further prove her musical fanaticism—and make us the biggest freaks in all of Lilly Pulitzer–wearing Winnetka—almost every wall of our house is plastered with photos of Bebe and her now-aging idols. Autographed ticket stubs, T-shirts, and a bass round out the mix. The absolute kicker is in the family room: a drum set–turned–coffee table signed by all of Dexy's Midnight Runners. Whoever they were.

Whenever my friends come over for the first time, it's always a big freak-out until they realize they have no idea who or what they're really looking at. It's always, "Is that Slash from Guns N' Roses with your mom in this picture?"

And I say, "Nope, it's Billy Squier."

Then they say, "Who?"

And I tell them, "Never mind."

Next they study the autographed bass. "Whoa. Nikki Sixx signed this?"

And I say, "Actually, Keith Scott did."

Then they say, "Who?"

He played with Bryan Adams, but they don't need to know that. Instead, I tell them, "If you don't know now, you never will."

Finally, they spot the drum set/coffee table. "Don't even ask," I say before they get totally confused.

Though I normally dreaded this whole routine, I thought I might actually enjoy running through it for Zander. I prayed to the ancient third-string rock gods he would come over for a visit soon.

Meanwhile, he was right next to me in the present tense, trying to make small talk. "You know what? We have a lot in common."

"We do?"

"Yeah. For one thing, we're both into running."

You could have fooled me, I thought. I just watched you and it wasn't pretty. "You're a natural," I said. Obviously, my brain was working just fine—it was only my mouth that refused to let all the good lines out.

"And music. We both love music." Zander gave me a slightly crooked smile that reminded me of Ashton Kutcher's. I was getting sucked in despite the fact I'd sworn off guys just last month. "I'm in a band. Want to hear us play sometime? Maybe you could sing backup or something."

"Ha-ha." I dug my fingernails into my arm really hard, just to make sure I wasn't dreaming. Red half-moons appeared, proof positive I was awake.

"If you're afraid of being alone with me and the guys, you could bring a friend along," he said. "C'mon, I don't bite. Not unless you want me to."

"I might be able to arrange that," I said, hoping I

sounded sexier than I must have looked, with the sweat dripping down my face and all.

"Maybe later," he said, flirting like crazy. "After you've showered. So, do you go to Northshore Regional?"

"Yup. You?"

Zander looked slightly embarrassed. "Nope. Country Day."

"Ahhhhh. One of them." Them unbelievably rich people, I meant. Yikes. This guy was so out of my league, I might as well quit now while I was ahead. "Well, gotta run, Zander. Nice meeting you."

He reached out and put his hand on my shoulder to stop me. "You haven't even told me your name yet."

Finally, something I could answer without feeling the need to be clever and witty. "Trace. Short for Tracey."

"So, Trace," Zander said, twirling my name around in his mouth. "You want to come see my band play at the rec center on Friday night or what?"

It was time to admit it: Wild horses couldn't keep me away. "Sounds good, Zander." My tongue must have swollen to gigantic proportions over the past few minutes, because it came out sounding like "Zounzgoozandah."

If he noticed, he didn't mention it. "Hey, in case you don't make it, what's your last name?"

"Tillingham," I said, my tongue returning to its normal size instantaneously.

I started the short run home, making it a full block before I gave in to my screaming mind and turned around for one last look at Zander. By then he was peanut-sized. Figures he'd pick now to turn into a gazelle, I thought.

"Good run?" the back of Bebe's head asked me as I banged through the front door. My mom's face was buried in the computer screen, as usual.

"Great one. I just met the hottest guy from Country Day."

Bebe twirled around in her chair and stopped working on whatever her latest novel was going to turn out to be. "Someone who can cure the T. J. blues?" T. J. was my last boyfriend—the one who dumped me for that slut Claire Russell the day after declaring his undying love for me.

"Could be. It's too early to tell."

"Gonna see him again?"

"Yup. He invited me to watch his band play Friday night."

"Hey, maybe I'll come along!"

I crinkled up my nose at the thought of it. "I don't think so. Not only would that mortify me, but they don't play oldies. Not your style at all, Bebe."

"I'm too cool to be mortifying," she said, clearly delusional. "And Duran Duran is playing the House of Blues, anyway. They can probably still blow the doors off your new boyfriend's band."

"Probably," I said, though I sincerely doubted it was true. I grabbed a water bottle from the frig and took a chug, wondering if Bebe even realized what a musical time warp she was in.

The Principles of Love

by Emily Franklin

Just to get this out of the way: yes, it's my real name. And no, I wasn't born on a commune (not unless you consider Boston, Massachusetts, circa 1989, to be a commune). In the movie version of my life, there'd be some great story to go with how I got my name—a rock star absentee father who named me in his hit song, or a promise my real father made to his grandmother in the old country. At least a weepy love story of two people so happy about their daughter they had to give her my name. But there's not—there's just me.

Love. My name is Love. Maybe this makes you think of your first kiss (mine = Jared Rosen, who managed to knock out my top left tooth at the beginning of the summer and provide my first kiss—a peck—by August's end). Or maybe you cringe when I introduce myself, wondering if I come complete with a tacky poster of cuddly kittens tangled in wool (I had one in third grade that showed a tabby clawing the wall, saying HANG IN THERE! Thank God for paper recycling).

Trust me: Despite what my name conjures up, I am not the sort to have a bed piled with fluffy kitties or well-loved stuffed animals. I actually don't even like cats all that much, not since I hugged little Snowball, my old neighbor's cat, right before the freshman formal last year and wound up sucking down antihistamines and nursing facial hives in my gown. Not pretty.

Then again, pretty's not all it's cracked up to be—or so I hear. I'm not what you'd call pretty, not the even more tantalizing *beautiful,* though maybe I've got potential. Right now I suppose I could fall into the category of appealing. My Aunt Mable's always saying the girls who peak in high school show up looking downright average at their tenth reunion, so I'm hoping (hoping = counting on) that my best years are still ahead of me. I don't want to look back on my life and have sophomore year of high school stand out as a blue ribbon winner, though the chances of that happening are slim at best. Part of me wouldn't mind trading places with the shiny, perfectly blond and still summer-tanned girls who probably emerged from the womb with a smile as wide as a Cadillac and legs from a music video. But since my life isn't one of those Disney movies where the heroine gets to swap places for a day and learn the secret to life, I have to be content to know only what it's like in my own life—and all I can say is it's too soon to tell.

We've been here (here = the Hadley Hall campus) for four days. Four days and six hours. And still not one decent conversation, not one promising smile-nod combination over mushy tuna sandwiches and lemonade outside, courtesy of FLIK, the school food supplier. When my dad told me about orientation for Hadley, I guess I imagined days spent lounging on the quad, soaking up the last of the summer rays while meeting cute boys, bonding with my two amazingly cool new best friends, and somehow forgetting that I have a forehead label—New Girl. Love, the New Girl. And not only that (here I'm imagining some lowly freshman pointing me out as someone who's even more lost than they are); I have the privilege of being the principal's daughter.

When my dad and I arrived on campus, typical trunk loaded with boxes, laundry hamper filled with my still-dirty duds, some overly enthusiastic tour leader showed us to the faculty housing. I followed my dad up the slate pathway toward the front door of a yellow Victorian house. Huge and with a wraparound porch, the house overlooks the playing fields and the rest of main campus. I stared at it, thinking of the card my dad gave me for my seventh-grade birthday—one of those 3-D cards that you unfold into a whole building—a large house with a turret and a carousel. I used to stare into that card as if I could get sucked into its landscape and experience some magical life for a while. This is what I thought of when I saw our new digs, minus the merry-go-round.

"This is Dean's Way," the tour guide boy explained, his hands flailing as he pointed out the features of our new abode—porch, view of central campus, door knocker in the shape of a heart. I stared at the metal heart and wondered for a minute if this could be an omen (heart=love=me) but then I rolled my eyes at myself. I hate when I give myself Lifetime programming moments.

"This is for you," Tour Guide said and handed my dad a large manila envelope and reached out to shake my hand. It still feels weird to shake hands as an almost-sixteen-year-old (almost = just under eight weeks until I'm highway-legal). Plus, Tour Guide never even asked my name. Around here, I guess I'm just a faculty brat.

My dad took the keys from the envelope (an envelope

labeled, by the way, PRINCIPAL BUKOWSKI AND DAUGHTER, as if I have no other identity), and began to fumble with the front door lock.

"Ready?" he asked, and smiled at me.

I nodded, excited. Dad and I have lived in some pretty grim places before—the apartment on Yucca Street that lived up to its name, the rent-reduced properties on the campus of Seashore Community College—so I never planned on living large. We've moved around a fair bit, actually, and one of the reasons Dad signed the contract with Hadley Hall was to make sure we could stay in one place. The thought of living here, of calling this home, or not peeling up anyone's old apartment buzzer labels and slicking ours on top, feels both comforting (stability = good) and trapping (sameness = confining)—or maybe I just mean revealing.

Dad rushed in, ever eager to explore new places and see what problems (kitchen bulb out, bed in the wrong place for optimum light) he might fix. That's what he does, problem-solve and rearrange. Me, I'm more cautious. I lurked for a minute in the doorway, holding onto the heart knocker and wondering what I'd find.

And I don't just mean that I stood there wondering what my new bedroom would look like. It was like right then, at the front door, I knew everything had changed—or would change, or was changing. The morphing process of leaving freshman year and the already hazy memories that went with. Soon, sophomore year at Hadley Hall—*the* Hadley Hall, with its ivy-coated brick and lush green lawns, its brood of young achievers, lacrosse-playing boys, and willowy girls—would begin. And I'd be in it.

In the made-for-television movie of this day, I'd wake up in my new house and while sipping my milky coffee, I'd meet my new best friend. We'd bond over loving the same sappy lyrics to 1970s songs (example = "Brandi (You're a Fine Girl)"—lame but awesome song from sometime in the late seventies). Then, later, I'd be getting ready to go for a jog (and by jog I mean slow, but hey-—it's something), and the Kutcher-esque hot guy I saw yesterday by the track would happen to be running by and take time out of his exercise regime to give me a guided tour of campus . . . and of himself. Heh. Unlikely—but then, it's a movie.

The reality of my life is this:

Outside, I can hear the buzz of bugs and the grunts from soccer and field hockey players from the fields near the house. I am decidedly unmotivated to get out of my bed—even though it's eleven o'clock. Last night, I caught my second, third, and fourth winds and wound up flipping stations between a *90210* rerun on cable and some infomercial that nearly convinced me to order that bizarre brush/hair-dye combo thing that supposedly makes it easy to home-color. Not that it'd be useful for me, since my hair is different enough already: penny-hued, with some bright bits at the front (not so suitable for highlights or lowlights—more like dimlights). I think about adding some wild streak of blue or something, but mainly this is when I'm PMSy. As my Aunt Mable always says, Let No Woman Attempt Hair Change When Hormonally Challenged. This was, of course, after the Miss Clairol mishap that took her three trips to the salon to correct.

Actually, I kind of pride myself on never having ordered from TV before—not that there's a fundamental flaw with it, but there's a principle there. Maybe I feel like if I started, there'd be no turning back, and pretty soon I'd wind up with that weird mop and the orange goop that strips paint and the hair-braiding contraption that I know would create such tangles I'd need to cut off great lops of hairs. So I avoid potential psychological damage (and smelly fumes) by refraining from any and all made-for-TV offers.

Plus, Aunt Mable already signed me up for the Time-Life Singer's & Songwriters discs. They arrive each month. She wants to edu-ma-cate me on the finer decades of rock and folk, long before OutKast and Britney. Most of the songs sound like an advertisement for deodorant, but I love the cheesiness of the lyrics, the mellow strumming of the guitars. Instead of John Mayer introspection, there's just old-fashioned lust or odes to seventies fashion. Half the time the guy's singing about making it with his lady or the woman's crooning about how her disco man done her wrong—what's not to appreciate there? Plus, sometimes Aunt Mable will listen with me and tell me how a particular song makes her think of being a cheerleader, eating grilled cheese, and making out with Bobby Stanhope in the back of his Camero.

With so much late-summer sunshine streaming in my window, I can't stay in bed any longer. It's harder to be a lazy slob in warm weather—hiding under the covers is much more gratifying in winter or heavy rains. I slide out of bed and onto the floor, pressing PLAY so I can hear the latest disc—it arrived yesterday, my first piece of mail to this new address. The typed label proved that I don't even need a street number anymore—just my name, Hadley Hall, Fairfield, Massachusetts, and the ZIP. Fairfield is "just outside Boston"—that's how the school catalog describes it, although my dad and I clocked it in the car and it's nearly twenty-four miles, so it's not as if you can walk it. Probably because of my own moniker, I am name-focused and tend to overanalyze place-names, so when my dad announced ("Love, pack your bags—we're going to prep school!" as if he'd have to endure the mandatory school blazer with me) we were moving to Fairfield, I couldn't help but picture green expanses and fair maidens traipsing along in long dresses, books carried by the same guy who'd throw his blazer over a mud puddle for easy-stepping.

Anyway, I was partially right. Fairfield is easy on the eyes, as are most of the Hadley students I've seen so far. Doing my usual shower routine, lathering all parts and hair while lip-synching, I wonder for a minute what life would be like here if the town were called "Hellville" or "Zitstown"—but when I emerge, clean and wet, and wipe the steam from the window, I can still see the soccer players and beautiful full elm trees. No ugliness here.

"She's going to be here any minute," my dad yells up from his post in the kitchen. I know his routine so well that I can tell he's already come back from the gym eaten the first half of his multigrain bagel. He doesn't use jam, he squashes fresh fruit onto the bread and munches away. He will have already set aside the last cup of coffee for me in the microwave, which he will nuke for forty-six seconds prior to my arrival in the kitchen. We have a system. It's what happens when you live with just one parent—either you don't know each other at all or you're way too familiar.

"Hey," I say, right as the microwave beeps to signal my caffeine is ready.

"Big shopping day?" Dad asks. He flips through a book. I shrug. I'm not Prada-obsessed or anything, but I enjoy looking around at what's out there. Mainly, it's an excuse to get off campus and be with Aunt Mable, who gives me regular reality checks.

"What's that?" I lean over his shoulder. Dad smells like strawberries and the original Polo from the green bottle. Dad smell. "Or, better yet, *who* is that?" The book in front of him contains black and white photos.

Dad puts on his game-show announcer voice, "The Faces of Hadley Hall!" I reach for the book. He holds it back and says in a regular voice, "I'm just trying to familiarize myself with the rest of the faculty. You'll get your own copy later in the year."

"And the IPSs?" (IPSs=Issue Prone Students—teacher code for screwups.)

"Maybe," Dad says and bites the rest of his bagel. "Eat something."

A car horn beeps. I can see Aunt Mable's car out the front window. She emerges from the driver's side and sits on the hood of the rusting black Saab 900. With jean cut-offs, black tank top, and Ugg boots the same camel color as her ringlets, Aunt Mable always looks like a rock star herself—Sheryl Crow's lost sister or something.

"I gotta go," I say. "You know I'll eat more than my fair

share with Mable. She's taking me on a culinary tour as well as showing me her personal fashion finds."

"Here," Dad hands me a key. "Your name here."

"My name here," I say back. This is our "I love you."

I take the house key and head outside. He could ask when I'll be home and I could answer that I don't know or make up some time frame, but the truth is, Dad doesn't set rules like that for me. He knows I'll call and tell him where I am and what I'm doing, and it's not a big enough deal to bother setting up some structure that I have to follow. Besides, I'm a lousy liar, and I never want to lie to him. It's his Jedi mind trick: He figures if he gives me enough freedom, I won't actually want it all. Here's the thing: Up till now, it's been true.

Before I even reach the Saab, my senses are overwhelmed. Mable's new carfume wafts from the rolled-down windows, and my aunt sits cross-legged on the hood of the car, singing along to Guns N' Roses ("Sweet Child o' Mine") at the top of her voice.

"Skipping decades?" I ask, and join in on the chorus.

"After you are thoroughly informed of the 1970s, you will pass Go and move on to obscure eighties tunes," she says.

"Axel Rose is not obscure," I say.

"True." She nods and slides off the hood to hug me. "But this is a classic."

Mable drives the twenty-four miles into Boston using back roads, and explains the various towns and subway stops along the way. We pass suburbs and slumburbs, a country club or two, industrial buildings, and a huge water tower splashed with brightly colored paints.

"Supposedly you can see faces and words in the mural," Mable says, pointing to the tower. "Personally, I think you can see Clapton's profile in the red part."

We make our way over Mass Ave., where hipsters and homeless people mingle. Passing by Berklee College of Music, I watch as students heft guitars, keyboards, and massive drums in the late summer heat. Aunt Mable watches me absorb the scene.

"Here we are, the mecca of vintage apparel," she says, sweeping her arm towards a store front like it's a new car on display.

"Baggy Bertha's?" I'm skeptical. Let me state that my own personal style is not fully developed. Not that I don't know what I like—I do, and I'm well aware of what makes me gag—but I'm sort of all over the place when it comes to picking out clothes. I have no trouble finding items that appeal (a pair of black flip-flops with plastic red flowers on them, faded Levi's 501s, two close-fitting tops—one electric blue, one layered white and gray), yet I have no idea how to put them together. It's like I'm a crow drawn to shiny things. After shopping I usually get home and sift through my purchases only to find there's not one presentable outfit in the lot. It's why I tend to stick to music instead.

"Perfect," Mable says of the suede jacket in front of her. "This, too. And let's try this."

She collects clothes, and I wander around the vintage shoe section, agog at the array of coolness and crap up for grabs. Next to thigh-high pleather boots (think Julia Roberts in the hooker phase of *Pretty Woman*) are Mary Janes and saddle shoes, Elton John disastrous sparkly clunkers circa 1976, and then—the black ankle boots I've longed for, like a riding boot only not in a dominatrix way. Plus, the heel would give me an extra couple of inches (I'm what the pediatrician called "on the smaller end of the growth chart"—better known as five-foot-two). I hold up my footwear find to Mable, who's clad in a bonnet and purple boa yet still manages to be sexy.

Mable makes me try on the Aerosmith–inspired Lycra outfit she's picked out, and I make her don a dress out of a fairy tale—not a Drew Barrymore kind of fairy tale; the Little Bo Peep kind. We stand in front of the three-way mirror, looking at the flipside images of ourselves.

"I'll never be this kind of rock star," I say, toying with the fringe on the sleeves. Mable smoothes her frilly petticoat. "If I placed an online personals ad with this picture of myself, would I find the love of my life?"

As I wait for Mable to get changed, I look at the old posters for Woodstock (the real one, not the Pepsi-mudfest) and *The Rocky Horror Picture Show,* the framed black-and-whites of Mod girls in thick eyeliner and go-go boots standing by their Vespa scooters. Was life better then? More fun? Simpler? Sometimes I think of life-as-told-by-a-Robert-Doisneau poster (you know, the master of romantic photography, who took those pictures of people kissing in Paris or the woman walking down the street in Italy), and how the days must have felt—I don't know—bigger somehow, more important. But then, I know I'm fantasizing because in these imaginings, I'm never in high school or doing dishes or tying shoes. But even the posters of hippies hanging out in front of the Metropolitan sign in Paris seem cooler than the midriff-baring teens we passed near Harvard Square. Maybe the past is bound to seem better, because it's done with.

Reading my mind, Mable pays for my boots with cash, glances at the hippy posters, and says, "It wasn't any different than today." Then she tilts her head, reconsidering. "Okay—a little bit. No e-mail, lots of polyester, and too much patchouli and smoke."

Boots in hand, I suddenly wish I were someone who felt that back-to-school shopping were the start of the rest of her life. But I'm not. I can't help but think it'd be easier if I gained redemption or enlightenment with a new purchase, or that getting a cool outfit meant my year would work out. I think of my dad, fortysomething and still picking out his ties as if he were presidential, as if superficial coatings mattered.

"Hey, lighten up, Brick," Aunt Mable says. She calls me Brick when, in her opinion, I'm thinking too hard or weighing down an otherwise pleasant moment.

"Sorry," I say, shaking my head to shrug off my thoughts. I roll down my window, rest my arm on the door frame, and let the wind wash over me.

"Look at us. We're like that Springsteen song." Mable smiles. I don't have to ask which one. She means "Thunder Road." She mentions it all the time. She loves the line about not being a beauty but being okay just the same. I always wait for the one about how highways or roads can lead you in whatever direction you choose—forward or back, able to take you anywhere.

Just like that, I'm out of my small funk and say, "I can't wait to get my license."

"That's right! You should be practicing. Drive. Hop in."

We swap sides, and I attempt to drive standard in the highway hell better known as Downtown Boston (hell = one way meets merge meets six lanes and a blinking red = huh?). Once she's fairly certain I'm not going to kill or maim us, Mable starts a round of RLG.

RLG is the game we devised—basically a musical Magic 8-ball. The rules for playing Radio Love God are elementary (though open for discussion and warping depending on how desperate the situation). The idea stems from the fact that we all do those stupid little tests with ourselves like "If I get this wrapper-ball into the trash on the first shot, so and so will like me," or "If the song ends by the time the light turns green, I'll get the job." Sometimes the tests work, but of course the odds go down if you start doing the "It's 11:11, make a wish and touch something red" and then you wish to become Paris and Nicky's other sister (but, hey, if that's what you're wishing, you have other, worse, problems).

Anyway, to play RLG, you have the volume down and say something along the lines of "Whatever song comes on next is from __ to me," or "The next one is how my summer will go." We make sure the volume-down rule is strict, because otherwise you can sort of cheat and, in the middle of "Your Body Is a Wonderland" say, "Oh, by the way, this is from that campus hottie to me." And that's just plain wrong.

The best part of this slightly loser game is that you can

twist the lyrics to suit your particular situation. For example, even if it's an ad for Jolly Jingle Cleaners and you've stated that it's from your long-lost summer love, you could interpret "We'll clean you, steam you, get the wrinkles out" as "See, he's wiped the slate clean from when I kissed that other guy. He's steaming—meaning he's still hot for me, and the wrinkles of our relationship are gone." And then you can go home and e-mail said boy, only to humiliate yourself when he doesn't write back. It's brilliant fun.

Mable takes her turn playing RLG and is saddened when she asks how business will go tonight and the reply is "Alone Again, Naturally." Mable runs her own coffeehouse, Slave to the Grind, with comfy couches, a laptop lounge, and amazing lattes, so she's constantly surrounded by people. I couldn't take that much face time. I like my alone time—balanced, of course, with a good friend or conversation.

Mable lets me parallel park (parking = getting it on the second try!), and we go for greasy cheeseburgers and sweet potato fries, splitting a vanilla frappe (frappe = East Coast milkshake).

"Are you thinking about the scene in *Grease* when Olivia Newton-John and Travolta hide behind their menus in the diner?" Mable asks.

"No," I say, sliding two fries in my mouth, whole, and then using dentist office-speak for a minute. "Ibuzthinknboutthishotguy."

"What hot guy?" Mable asks. She has an uncanny ability to understand dentist-speak.

"Someone at Hadley. He's probably an idiot."

"A really gorgeous idiot?"

"Yeah, that. Plus, I was thinking how much I miss singing."

At my old school, I was in a band. Maybe not the best band, but Baby Romaine ("Baby," as in the girl from *Dirty Dancing* who won't be put in a corner, and "Romaine," as in lettuce, as in *let us* play—hey, it was freshman year) gave me an outlet aside from Mable's car and my shower for singing.

"Well, you've got an incredible voice. What about Hadley? There's got to be—what—an octet group or something . . . like in *American Pie*." Yet again, Mable references movies and songs to prove a point, but this one's lost on me.

"Yeah, I know. But I don't want that—"

She cuts me off. "Then write your own songs."

I want to protest or crack a joke, but I don't. I just eat my burger and nod. I'm so afraid of sounding cheesy in songs, or derivative, that even though words sometimes swirl in my head, I don't write them down.

Bartley's Burgers turns out to be this famous place. Harvard undergrads, former presidents, movie scouts on location, all come here for the grub. The walls are blanketed with peeling bumper stickers (ENVISION WHIRLED PEAS, ELVIS HAS LEFT THE BUILDING) and NO NUKES signs.

Mable sees me checking out all the paraphernalia and wipes her mouth on the little paper napkin. "Your mom and dad used to come here."

My hand freezes before my mouth, a quivering sweet potato fry stuck in midair. No one ever mentions my mother. Ever. Not even in passing.

"Sorry," Mable says and quickly slurps some frappe. "It was a million years ago."

By my quick calculations, Mable's overestimating by about 999,987. "No—wait—go back."

Mable shakes her head. "Never mind, it's late. I should drive you home."

"It's not home, it's Hadley," I say, annoyed at how teenagery I sound. "Seriously, Mable, I'm not being Brick, I just have to know something. Tell me anything."

"Fine." Mable takes a breath and looks around. "Once, I saw your parents sitting in that corner over there, sharing some sproutburger or whatever alfalfa mojo your mother liked then. Your dad drummed the table, as per usual. He's done that since we were kids. And your mom put her hand on his like this." Mable flattens her own fingers and leaves her hands resting on each other. "And . . ."

She looks at my face. Probably I look too eager, too desperate. She cuts herself off. "And that's all."

I open my mouth to demand further details, but Mable's gone up to pay the bill.

The car ride back to Hadley Hall starts off stilted, with no conversation, just the radio's declaration, over and over again, that summer is over. WAJS plays tributes to this effect, with songs talking about empty beaches and seasons changing. This, plus the sight of the Hadley campus makes me cloud up again.

Chin on my hand, I stick my face partway out the window like a dog. In front of the house—our house—my house—Mable stops the car.

"Listen—forget what I said back at Bartley's. Say hi to

215

your dad for me, and just enjoy the here and now." I know she's not just talking about movies and songs and decades-old hippy posters. She means forget the maternal mystery, don't dwell on what could be—just live in the present.

After dinner, I sit on the porch while my dad commits to memory student names from the face book. People here have names that seem more suitable to towns or buildings: Spence, Channing, Delphina, Sandford. I mean weren't Pacey and Dawson enough of a stretch?

Outside, I can't get comfortable—first too hot in my sweatshirt, then too cold in just my T-shirt. Then the porch slats cut into my thighs, so I stand up.

"It's less windy on the other side," says a voice from around the turret-edge of the house.

I go to discover the person to whom the voice is attached. Sitting on one of the white Adirondack chairs in the front of the house with her knees tucked up to her chest is:

"Cordelia, as in one of King Lear's daughters, and a fac brat just like you."

She rattles off other information—about me, my dad, the house (turns out the heart-shaped door knocker was put on by some old headmistress who died a spinster, so not a lot of romantic omen there).

"I'm Love," I say, even though Cordelia knows this already. And before she can make some joke about it, I add, "Bukowski. Love Bukowski."